Green Wings to Eden

PAUL GARVEY

"Birds do it and fly,
Bees do it and die,
Dogs do it and stick to it,
Let's do it, you and I."

I don't know who said it first, but Bob 'Giz' Garvey said it
most.

This one's for Ava.

ACKNOWLEDGMENTS

Thanks to everyone who read *Tomorrow's Sun* and let me know it might be worth hearing from me again. I hope I don't let you down. Thanks to Kunaal Sarna, Mark O'Regan, and Mike Raimondi for giving up their time to read earlier drafts of *Green Wings to Eden* and provide feedback. Your help is very much appreciated and hopefully made this a better book. Thanks to Domenic Papile for providing me insight into a day in the life of a Correctional Officer and to Matt Glynn, a most unexpected model, for lending his imposing silhouette for the original cover.

Finally a special thanks to my wife Elaine and daughter Ava. I'm not known for my charming personality to begin with, and I'm sure the late nights spent writing and accompanied lack of sleep make me slightly less pleasurable to be around. Your tolerance and support is immeasurable, thank you.

PROLOGUE

Andrew watched the tall reeds behind the school dance back and forth in the light summer breeze. He held a regulation sized basketball in between hands that looked too small for the rest of his body. Others in his grade had already seen growth spurts stretch out their limbs and began to speak in voices that cracked with early signs of puberty. Andrew's voice however, still had a child's pitch and his hands along with the rest of him still waited eagerly for any signs of extension. His father assured him that he'd also thin out his pudgy frame once he did grow taller.

He bounced the basketball off the ground in front of his feet, then stretched backwards extending his neck so that he could see everything behind him though his vision in that position showed everything upside down. He caught sight of the backboard and rim and judged their distance, then brought his head back right side up again. The blood had rushed to his head and he took a few seconds to regain his balance. When the dizziness wore off , he spun the ball gently in his hands and bounced it another time.

1

'Shoot the ball already!' his friend Stevie's voice yelled from underneath the basket. Andrew straightened up and took in a long breath, then blew it out slowly. He shut his eyes for a moment and tried to picture where the rim and basket were behind him. Then, he sailed the ball backwards over his head. He opened his eyes and turned towards the hoop in time to see the ball clank hard off the top of the backboard and out of bounds to the left. 'Shoot' he said to himself and kicked at a small patch of sandy pebbles that gathered in a crack at his feet.

Stevie chased the ball down laughing, 'ah ha' he yelled, 'you missed. That makes you H.O.R. You're a whore Andrew!'

'Yeah yeah Stevie. Okay' Andrew said back. He hated playing HORSE with Stevie because he had a knack for making trick shots that were nearly impossible to replicate.

'Nice try Andrew.' Bernie said from the swing set on the other side of the chain link fence. 'What do you mean?' Stevie yelled to her. 'He didn't even hit the rim!'

Andrew watched Bernie smile at him, then she turned and stuck her tongue out at Stevie. Stevie looked around him first to make sure no grown-ups were around then held up his middle finger. 'Ooooh' Bernie said 'I hope Ms. Cranston saw you from the window.' Then she turned and ran around the large slide and disappeared to the other end of the playground. Stevie didn't bother responding and walked back over to Andrew on the basketball court. 'I think somebody likes you Andrew.'

'Who? Bernie? No she doesn't.' Andrew said. He felt his face start to grow hot as he blushed. 'You're scared!' Stevie said and laughed. 'Just take your next shot Stevie, it's getting late.'

'Fine' he said and dribbled the ball to the top of the three-point line. He paused and judged the distance to the hoop, then walked further away to the edge of the court and turned towards the basket again. 'Okay! Underhanded from here!' he yelled to Andrew. 'That's all, nothing else.' Stevie crouched down low and held the ball with both hands between his knees. He jumped up from his low position and strained to bring his hands up with force to reach the basket. He let go of the ball sending it high in the air.

Andrew followed the ball from Stevie's hands into the air above his head then all the way to the rim. It hit the back of the rim and bounced away. He chased after the rebound and grabbed the ball before it rolled into the long grass and reeds beside the court.

He picked the ball up in two hands and started walking back towards the court. He noticed three people walking from the other side of the court approaching Stevie from the parking lot. He grew nervous at the sight of them. There was a tall boy in the center that wore a Red Sox hat pulled low with the rim curved so that it cut the ends of his eyebrows from view. The boy looked at least a couple years older than he and Stevie. Andrew thought he had to be at least thirteen or fourteen. He was book-ended by two smaller boys that looked closer to Andrew's age. Each wore plain white t-shirts and shorts. One of the smaller boys called out to Stevie. Stevie looked back at Andrew and shook his head slightly. Andrew guessed Stevie didn't know them either. They stopped in front of Stevie, but Andrew was too far away to hear if they were saying anything. He was nervous, but headed over towards them anyway, afraid to leave Stevie by himself. He'd heard of kids from neighboring parks going around to other schoolyards and starting trouble. It was only a matter of time before some ended up at theirs. Andrew had never been in a fight, but had heard stories from his older brother and his friends about how things happened. Although, it was still unclear to him why it happened at all.

Andrew continued towards the group and could hear them laughing as he approached. It was a mocking laughter, one he'd heard a few times in the schoolyard. 'Look at his shoes' one of the smaller boys said to the others while pointing at Stevie's sneakers. 'Little poor boy, can't afford real shell-toes! Look, he's got four stripes!' Andrew felt a

4

pang of anger. It was not the first time he'd heard someone pick on Stevie for how he looked. He seemed to draw insults often from other kids whose parents could afford things that Stevie's mother couldn't, like brand name sneakers. He looked over at Stevie. He wasn't saying anything back. Andrew could see Stevie's flaring nostrils take in air slowly and saw his eyes start to fill with moisture. He could feel his own heart beating rapidly in his chest and his vision started to fade in and out with red clouds forming in his periphery. 'Leave him alone!' he yelled. He could hear his own high pitched voice echo in the empty schoolyard. He wished his voice had come out deeper, but he couldn't control it. He watched as the three boys turned to him. The tall one with the baseball hat stepped closer to him. Andrew shifted his feet back slightly. 'What are you gonna do, you fat monkey?' the tall boy said. The two smaller boys broke out in laughter. Stevie slid back a couple feet so that he was shoulder to shoulder with Andrew.

'Why can't you just leave us alone?' Andrew said in a lower voice this time. The tall boy leaned in and said to Andrew, 'I was talking to your friend here, until you butted in. I saw him give that little girl the finger. I want to see him be a tough guy to me.'

'That was a joke!' Stevie pleaded. 'Bernie's our friend.' The tall boy stepped quickly towards Stevie and shot a hand out and smacked him in the face. Stevie fell backwards and struggled to get back to his feet. Andrew's vision faded in and out faster this time and the red from the edges ran quickly towards the center. He watched the tall boy turn and give each of the smaller boys high-fives. 'Go get them one of the hockey sticks.' The tall boy said. 'maybe then it'll be a fair fight.' Andrew fought to control his breathing, but couldn't any longer. He gripped the basketball in his hands tightly. He stepped forward and yelled 'Run Stevie!' Then he threw the basketball hard, a chest pass, right at the tall boy's face. The boy didn't expect it and it hit him square on the nose and blood shot out from his nostrils immediately.

Stevie took off running when Andrew yelled. After he threw the ball, Andrew took off behind him. Stevie had always been faster than Andrew and the head start meant he had already created distance between them. He saw Stevie look back at him. Andrew waved his hand forward twice yelling 'go!' as he did. Stevie had reached the side walk and turned left up the street. Andrew was barely at the edge of the parking lot and he could hear the footsteps and yells behind him gaining on him quickly. He was about to step off the curb when he felt a hand grab hold of his shirt. That same hand pushed him forward and with momentum carrying him already, he fell forward hard and slid across the cement. His palms and knees burned as they scraped across the hard gravel. When he stopped sliding, he rolled over onto his back. In less than a second the boys were upon him. He pulled his knees closer to his body and brought his arms up over his head and face. He could feel punches and kicks all over his body. Some hurt, like those that made it to his ribs or his face. Others, he felt the impact, but the pain didn't register. He tried looking up, but saw only a sea of fists flying at him. After that he kept his eyes shut. The pain seemed to fall into the background and his body grew numb. He felt slimy liquid crawl down his face that left a metallic taste in his mouth. He was starting to slip away, in and out of consciousness. He struggled to keep his arms up, but knew he had to keep his head covered. The fists and kicks kept coming. It felt like days had past as he lay there, crouching, trying to make his body tight. Then suddenly, he heard a 'thump'. Then it all stopped.

The punches and kicks stopped coming. He laid there still. He was afraid to open his eyes for fear of what he'd find. Perhaps the tall boy wanted to make him watch his own demise. He felt a hand lightly shake his shoulder and a familiar voice call out. 'Andrew. Andrew, you okay?' it asked. Andrew opened his eyes. The boys were gone. Stevie was crouched down next to him, rubbing his shoulder. Stevie took his t-shirt off and wiped down Andrew's face gently. 'Hold it tight against your cheek Andrew. You're bleeding.'

Andrew sat up slowly with Stevie's help. He felt around his face and could tell his eyes and lips were swollen. 'I thought you got away?' he asked Stevie. 'I did get away.'

'But, you came back?'

'Of course I did Andrew. They caught you. I thought they were gonna kill you. They wouldn't stop hitting you.'

'Where'd they go? How'd you get them to stop?'

Stevie took a seat on the ground next to Andrew and held his hands back to keep himself upright. He looked around the parking lot before answering. 'They ran off after I hit the big kid.'

'You punched him?' Andrew asked.

Stevie shook his head no. 'No. I didn't punch him. I didn't think that would work. I hit him with a stickball bat. The two other boys stopped hitting you then. The big kid tried to get up and come after me, so I hit him again. I hit him in the head Andrew . . . the others then, they dragged him away.'

'Jesus Stevie . . . you saved me.'

Stevie patted Andrew on the back gently. 'You stuck up for me. You would've done the same if they caught me.'

Andrew thought about it for a minute. He wasn't sure if he'd have done exactly the same, he was afraid. The fear might have frozen him, but he couldn't know for sure. He just nodded to Stevie. Stevie stood, then helped Andrew get to his feet slowly.

Andrew stood and began to walk slowly, leaning on Stevie's shoulder for support. He noticed the sky started to darken. It was late and he hoped he wouldn't get in trouble for staying out past dinner time. Then he thought about how he looked. He was obviously beat up. He began praying silently that his father and brother weren't home. He knew if they saw him in the condition he was now, they'd both drag him out to scour the streets for the boys that did it. All he wanted to do was get cleaned up and go to bed. They crossed the street and headed in the direction of Andrew's house. 'Where did you find the stickball bat?' Andrew asked Stevie after a couple minutes. 'It was leaning against the fence next to the playground.' Stevie answered. 'I saw it when I ran back to the parking lot.' 'Lucky for me.' Andrew said. 'Yeah, but not for that big kid.' Stevie said.

They didn't say much the rest of the walk to Andrew's house. When they reached the block before his, Andrew could sense Stevie's question coming. At least three or four nights a week during the summer Stevie would hint around or just flat out ask Andrew if he could ask his parents to let him stay the night. He never wanted to go home it seemed. Andrew didn't mind, but he could tell it irritated his parents sometimes, especially his father for some reason. It got to the stage that most of the time, Andrew would just go inside and pretend to ask his parents, then come out and tell Stevie that they said 'not tonight.' However, after Stevie had saved his life pretty much, he felt he owed him enough to actually ask his mother this time.

Stevie and Andrew walked into the house together. When Andrew's mother saw them first, she was obviously upset at Andrew's appearance and let both boys know it. She calmed after a minute however and went and got Stevie a spare t shirt and pair of shorts to change into. Then she took Andrew into the bathroom and washed down his face and cleaned his cuts with peroxide. Stevie waited in the living room and watched television.

'Who did this to you Andrew?' She asked several times, but Andrew kept telling her that it was three boys, but he didn't know them, which was true. She finally gave up asking, but said, 'You're very lucky your father isn't home. Best stay out of his sight until the morning, or else he'll have you all around the city tonight hunting for these boys.' 'I know Mum' was all he could say. 'Do you mind if Stevie stays over tonight?' he asked. His mother finished dabbing his cuts with peroxide on a cotton ball and threw the cotton, now covered in blood, into the trash bin. 'Again Andrew?' she asked.

'I know Ma, but he did risk his neck for me today. Maybe

next time I can stay at his house.'

His mother grabbed his shoulders firmly with both hands and looked straight at Andrew. She said in a hushed voice, 'He can stay tonight Andrew. But listen, I don't want you going over to Stevie's house. And I especially don't want you staying overnight there do you hear me?'

Andrew stared back at her and just nodded his head. 'Yeah, fine, okay Mum, but . . . why?' he asked. 'Just promise me you won't . . . someday you'll understand.' She answered. Andrew didn't know how to respond. He didn't know what she meant or why it mattered so much to her. He felt awkward all of a sudden and grew claustrophobic in the small bathroom. 'Fine.' He said.

He got up and walked out of the bathroom into the narrow hallway towards the living room. Outside the living room he stood in front of a mirror that hung at eye level on the wall. He squinted to look at his reflection using the dim light from the television. His face looked clean now, but his eyes and lips were both swollen badly. He thought he could already see a bruise forming around the outside of his left eye, all the way down the left side of his face. He looked away from the mirror and walked into the living room. 'You can stay over tonight Stevie' he said. There was no response. He saw the television flashing in the background with a sports highlight show playing. The television's volume was turned all the way down. He walked over to the set and switched it off. He looked down at the couch, which had Stevie stretched out across it, already lightly snoring in a deep sleep. Andrew stretched out the blanket that draped over the end of the couch and pulled it over Stevie's feet and up to his torso. 'Goodnight Stevie' he said softly, then reached behind the couch and switched off the last remaining lamp in the room.

CHAPTER ONE

The grey dawn of winter in the northeast grew monotonous by the time March arrived. An overcast sky with heavy snow clouds primed to release logistical hell were nearly a reason to smile in late December. Even the familiar blizzard during the short days of February weren't cause for concern. By March however, the novelty wore off. Men and women battled bouts of seasonal depression, while school kids, once taken with snow days spent sledding at the golf course, shivered at the possibility of extending the school year late into June. An abbreviated summer was a high price to pay for any winter day off.

Andrew Dawson sat quietly in his truck listening to sports talk radio. Every weekday for years he sat in that very spot, struggling to keep his eyes open, waiting for his best friend and partner Stevie Black to show up. They drove together every day, 'well, I drive him every day, he sits there and messes with my radio' Andrew thought. The meeting spot was always the same, the small front parking lot of West Elm Variety, a convenience store on a side street off of Wollaston Beach. The meeting time was always the same too, six thirty am. Although Stevie's zest for spontaneity often dictated exactly the time they met, sometimes earlier, but mostly later, unless it was pay day. The promise of a pay check always got Stevie out of bed before the alarm clock went off. West Elm Variety was the midpoint between Andrew and Stevie's childhood homes. It's where they met every morning before walking to school together. After high school, both men went to work as apprentice carpenters for the same company. They hung on to the habit of meeting outside the store, even though neither lived in his childhood home any longer.

Andrew waited patiently in his old Ford pickup truck. His eyes watered and nose was dried up from the defrost pumping hot air relentlessly at his face. Every time he turned it down, he struggled to fight off the chill that quickly settled in his bones. The cold air was let in by the rickety old truck's loose insulation. Also, the windscreen seemed to steam up immediately once the dial was turned off. The truck was weighted down with racks in the back and a retro-fitted lock box for tools, plus a solid foot of wet snow that had fallen overnight. Despite his six foot two, two-hundred and thirty pound frame, Andrew never did grow accustomed to fifty hour weeks of physical labor. The toll his body had taken in his short career made him feel double his age.

He reached into the center cup holder and picked up a pill bottle. He held it up to the windscreen towards the street lights and gave it a shake to see if he could count how many pills remained. After a recent slip from a ladder that resulted in a pulled back muscle, a doctor prescribed him some high dosage Ibuprofen. He was nearly through his final refill, but the pain had yet to subside. The clock above his tape deck showed six forty-nine am. Andrew checked his phone to confirm. 'Yup, almost twenty minutes late, come on Stevie' he said to himself. Outside, the sky was still a charcoal grey and the snow remained steady, looking like specs of volcanic ash in contrast to the dim early day light. Andrew's Ford was the lone vehicle in the front lot, but he was surprised to see a slow trickle of pedestrians enter and exit the store in the last twenty minutes, each time hearing the chime of the door's bell faintly through the noise of the heat and the sound of the engine.

To give his tearing eyes a rest, he reached over and switched the heat off, slightly unnerved by the sudden silence once the monotonous hum was broken. He tried to breathe slowly so his windows wouldn't fog up, but within a minute the condensation blocked his view through the windscreen. He ducked his head and reached under the passenger seat for a sponge that he kept to wipe down the windows. When he finally got his hand on it, he stretched over the steering wheel and ran it across the windscreen. When his line of sight was cleared, something strange caught his eye inside the store. From the outside it looked like there was an animated conversation going on between the customer and the clerk. The clerk was a man Andrew grew up with called Chef Benson. Andrew cleared more of the window quickly with both hands now and peered through the glass. The customer wore a wool hat pulled low and a hooded sweatshirt. He was clearly pointing to something repeatedly, which appeared to be the register. Chef was only slightly visible from the street. Most of his frame was hidden behind promotional signs for Bud Light thirty packs plastered on the window. From what Andrew could see, he looked to be shaking his head frantically as if saying no.

Andrew's hands gripped the steering wheel tightly and without realizing, he'd pulled his body off the seat, tighter to the dash, his chest nearly resting at the wheel's twelve o'clock. He saw the customer lunge forward over the counter towards Chef, swinging at him with his right hand in a closed fist. Chef tried to jump back, but with limited space behind the counter, he couldn't move out of the way and the punch landed square on his temple. Andrew saw him fall to the ground. The thief then jumped forward again, this time reaching over the counter, for what Andrew assumed was the cash register. He pulled back his arm and his hand carried a fist full of bills. The man stuffed his hands into the pockets of his hoodie and turned and ran out of the front door.

Outside the door, the man paused at the top of the steps, startled to see Andrew standing in the parking lot staring at him. From instinct, Andrew had opened his door and jumped down from the truck to the pavement. Both men stopped in his tracks as they made eye contact with one another. They stood staring in silence for a few seconds, looking like a paused video game. Finally, the thief made a step towards the stairs only to quickly change direction and shoot the other way down the handicapped ramp. Andrew bit on the fake and slipped on the slushy ground when he tried to recover and change direction. The thief quickly made it down the ramp and with Andrew down in a pile of wet snow and slush, used the truck for leverage. He ran quickly around the truck bed and took off running towards Wollaston Beach.

Andrew got up clumsily and started in an attempted sprint after the man. As he did, he heard Chef Benson calling after him from outside the store. Andrew's feet moved as quickly as possible, pounding furiously through the snow on the un-shoveled sidewalk. He jumped off the curb and onto the street, which was slightly improved thanks to the early morning snow plows. He continued running through the street and after a final sprint towards the corner, he slid to a stop as if on ice skates. He looked across Quincy Shore Drive to the beach wall, unwilling to risk life and limb by darting aimlessly across the busy street. He pulled his wool hat off and looked left down the street, then right, searching in the distance for any sign of the thief or his footsteps. He saw nothing but white flakes in each direction as the snow continued to fall steadily like a shaken snow globe. He looked to the sky and let a couple flakes fall on his tongue before leaning forward with his hands on his knees while trying to slow his breathing and assess the level of pain now bursting from his back.

Andrew turned away from the beach after catching his breath for a minute and began a slow trod back down the street towards his truck. His walk was slow and deliberate with the piercing pain coming from his back muscles. Every step carried with it chronic discomfort. His hair had gotten wet with sweat from the run and mixed with the heavy snow flakes that continued to fall relentlessly. He shivered from the cold and put his wool hat back on his head as he trudged through the mess. He stared down the road surprised at the distance he had covered in his sprint. Through the peppering snow he saw a truck's familiar grill and headlights accompanied by its laboring engine. As the truck grew near, it grew more familiar as well. When it pulled to a stop next to him, Andrew shook his head at the driver in disapproval. 'Stevie' he said, 'I thought I was clear on my ground rules. You're not to drive my truck except for in cases of extreme emergencies.' Stevie had reached across the passenger seat to push the door open and heard him clearly. 'Listen guy, just be glad it's me driving this piece of shit.' Stevie answered, 'Who leaves their frigin car running anymore? You're lucky it's shitty out, this thing was a sitting duck outside the store. Forget unlocked, the damn door was wide open and the keys were in it. What's wrong with you?'

Andrew walked tenderly into the street, trying to keep his balance while stepping down from the curb to the glazed pavement. He reach the passenger door and pulled it open further. He lifted himself up onto the seat, grimacing in pain as he did.

Stevie noticed his change in facial expression and asked, 'Back still at you?'

'Yeah, a little. I think I might've tweaked it running down the street after that guy.'

'Well, serves you right chasing after school kids you creep.'

'Fuck you Stevie, I witnessed a robbery for chrissakes. I was chasing after the guy.'

'Yeah, I know' Stevie said 'I saw you take off down the street and Benson filled me in briefly as he made my coffee.' Stevie reached down and pulled up a white Styrofoam cup and held it to his lips, blowing gently at the steam coming out of the top as he did.

'You bastard' Andrew said 'you stopped for coffee when I was trying to make a citizen's arrest? What if I caught the dude and he had a weapon or something?'

Stevie took a delicate sip from the hot cup, then looked over back at Andrew. 'Seems like something you should've considered before you ran after him huh?'

Andrew just shrugged in reluctant agreement. 'Yeah you're probably right. But, still man.'

'Don't worry' Stevie answered as he finally put the truck back into drive and slowly rolled forward. 'You weren't ever going to catch that guy. That dude was a vampire man. He was all whacked out. You were running through that thick snow, he might as well have been floating across it. Plus, you ain't exactly known for your foot speed.'

Andrew just rolled his eyes and sat back into the passenger seat, willing to let Stevie drive since the pain in his back limited his reaction time anyway. 'Which I'd need in this weather' he thought. Although he began to reconsider as the unmistakeable waft of stale booze crept past his nostrils once the windows were up and doors were closed. 'You out somewhere last night Stevie?' he asked nervously while trying to sound casual. He wanted to avoid Stevie getting defensive, 'a mode he seemed to default to these days' Andrew thought.

'Might've been. Why, who's asking, my priest?'

'Nah man, just uh . . . making conversation that's all. But man, I hate to break it to you, you are giving off a werewolf scent.' Andrew answered and smiled trying to keep the inquisition light. 'You're cool to drive though right? Last thing we need is a DUI between us.'

Stevie's face flashed with irritation, much like that of a child being reminded of his homework. 'I'm perfect Andrew.' He answered 'You want me to pull over or something? Last thing I want is to crash your piece of shit truck.'

The air between the two men grew stale quickly. This was also becoming common place on their journeys to work and usually led to neither speaking to the other, at least not until boredom took its toll, which generally meant by lunchtime. Andrew decided to back down and try to salvage peace for the long day ahead of them. 'No Stevie, keep driving, you got it. Sorry I even brought it up.'

Stevie said nothing else in reply and seemed to just focus

on the road. Andrew noticed his grip on the steering wheel tighten ever so slightly. He glanced up at Stevie's face trying not to be noticed while staring. He thought about the distance between them that seemed to develop out of nowhere in recent months, 'Maybe it was even longer than that' he considered, like a virus that had laid dormant and imperceptible until it was too late. 'Nah' he thought after a minute 'It's just a bad patch, even the closest of friends can get sick of each other. It's probably just over exposure.'

Andrew's thoughts drifted away from Stevie as he cleared the fog from his window with his sleeve. He watched the snow as it continued falling. It had gotten heavier than before and seemed to be mixing now with rain as the temperature started to rise with daybreak. He began to focus on the eight hours of work ahead of him. He felt dread thinking about the coldness that would embed itself into him by dinner time. With that thought he switched the heat back on high to let the noise from the radiator drum out his thoughts and laid his head back and shut his eyes to rest before facing the day.

CHAPTER TWO

Working on a house in South Boston was like the carpenter's equivalent of getting a grenade handed to you with the pin already pulled. For starters, the houses were either attached or at least too close together. That meant any job that involved outside work, had you wedged between buildings like a dinosaur trying to walk through the Gothic District in Barcelona. While any inside renovation had you equally cramped into spaces built for under-nourished nineteenth century immigrants. Add to the mix the steep staircases and snow falling outside and Andrew could barely move his limbs by the end of his day, let alone drive home.

His morning consisted of replacing windows on every floor of the narrow four-story town house, while the afternoon had him hanging vinyl siding in the crevice that was the side of the house. By the end of the day, every inch of his body ached and his hands burned from the over exposure to the wet snow and cold wind that swept through the alleyway. At home, he let the hot shower rain over him for twenty minutes. His skin flushed with red and stung with pain afterwards, but he felt it was worth it to rid the cold from his bones.

Andrew's apartment was small, but it was tidy. His bedroom seemed spacious, but that had more to do with his lack of furniture than the actual size of the room. There was a spare bedroom, but it looked more like a walk-in closet with a futon in it. His visitors were scarcely overnight guests. The living room was small, but functional with a basic couch and old television that echoed that same sentiment. His kitchen was what realtors called a kitchenette, but more realistically should be described as a closet with an oven in it.

Andrew dried off in the bathroom and got dressed in the spare room that housed most of his clean clothes. His laundry always got washed and dried, but for some reason he could never find the time, energy or inclination to put it away.

He took his time getting ready. He felt exhausted from the week's work and although he managed to shake off the chill from earlier, his face and hands still suffered from chaffing due to the unseasonable cold that plagued the east coast. He put on his best pair of going-out jeans and found a button-down shirt that didn't need ironing. He hadn't bothered to shave that morning, but usually he kept the grizzled look anyway, which he always felt took a few pounds off his face. He pulled out all the stops for his hair, broke out the expensive pomade that left a slightly slick shine through his dark mane. Lastly he gave his shirt and neck a mist of cologne before pulling on a brown pair of boots and grabbing his jacket.

He walked down his steps and outside to his truck. He put the keys into the driver-side door to unlock it, feeling awkward, even without an audience, a man trying to be spruced up, yet walking into a beat up old pickup. He imagined the sight of him dressed in his going out attire standing next to his sad truck was on par with putting cologne on a pig.

He slid into the driver's seat and started up the old Ford. The snow had stopped falling during the day and the evening was bright, which seemed to hasten the return of spring. The streets throughout the day also melted, but the road salt lingered, wreaking havoc on the undercarriage of unsuspecting automobiles, its presence on the road now at odds with the balmy evening.

Andrew's hands burned from splits that developed while working outside in the cold. He loosened his grip on the steering wheel to ease the pain that accompanied the cracks around his fingernails. Also, his back had continued to ache, surely exacerbated by the day's physical labor. When he got home from work, he wanted so badly to stay there in his apartment, shower, get the sweats on and just watch TV. However, Stevie had mentioned earlier that day that Bernadette was planning to be around that night.

All throughout high school and for the first few years afterwards, Bernadette had been his girlfriend. They were on again, off again, but for the most part during that time, they were together. She had been his first love and he was hers, at least he had hoped he was. In fact, Andrew knew she was the only girl he had ever loved. There was no one before and had been no one really after. He'd gone out with a few woman since, but no one consistent and no one that tugged at his heart strings like she did.

At times, he felt that he was under a spell, as if cupid himself followed him around and shot arrows in his ass every time he saw her. She was beyond gorgeous, especially in his eyes, though he never needed to ask anyone else's opinion. She looked like no one else he'd ever encountered, at least not in person. Her hair was red, well, more strawberry blonde, and her eyes were a dark blue. Her skin was fair, but seemed to always have a hint of color and her freckles, although faint, were unmistakable. Since the first time he laid eyes on her, he felt a stirring in his stomach whenever she was near. 'I can't even believe she was mine for years' Andrew thought, not in a sense that he owned her, but in a way they were connected, a ying to Andrew's yang.

As young love often did, theirs had grown apart over time. Once so connected and invested in each other, their lives both came to a point where it made sense to move on. She wanted to try somewhere new, a fresh start, so she went away to college. Andrew knew he couldn't live with himself if he'd held her back. Plus, after high school he ran into hard times with family issues, ones that he still couldn't bear to confront.

Bernadette went to Syracuse in New York. It wasn't a million miles away, but it was far enough. Eventually after school, she did move back to Massachusetts, but not Quincy. She moved in with a young business man from Philadelphia, to his house in a town called Boxford. It was a small town miles outside of Boston, almost in New Hampshire. Andrew had looked the place up when he'd heard. It was a tiny place north of Boston with less than ten thousand people. All he knew of it was that it was formerly farmland and it still had cows there. He'd heard it was nice and peaceful, it sounded so anyway.

Since then, her visits back to Quincy were not very frequent, and they were usually on Sundays just to visit her parents. The odd time she'd appear on a Friday or Saturday night in their local bar, Mackin's Saloon, or down in Marina

Bay during the summer. If Andrew heard only after the fact that she was around and he'd missed her, he'd be miserable for weeks. Luckily Stevie saw a post on Facebook during the day and mentioned to him that she might be around that night. So Andrew, who originally just wanted his bed, decided to go out, just in case she was around. Time had passed and they were no longer an item, but there was still something between them, a flicker of hope maybe. Andrew felt it at least. He hoped he wasn't the only one.

CHAPTER THREE

Mackin's Saloon was a neighborhood bar. The small building sat on a street corner at the bottom of a residential hill that ran into a main street leading to the highway. Its location was outside of the town center, which lended to its reputation of a locals bar. It was enough out of the way that no one really went there by accident. The heavy wooden door at the entrance looked like some antique piece of drawbridge pulled from a castle's ruins. Inside that herculean door was an Irish bar in the purest sense, not made to look like one, but one which others would later be fashioned. The floors had to be changed every few years due to the foot traffic, and the drop ceiling had to be replaced after the smoking ban came into effect. However, everything else pretty much withstood the test of time.

Andrew liked the place because he could always rest assured he'd run into friends there or at least like-minded strangers he could blow off steam with. Plus, the first round on Fridays was on the house for regulars and the Guinness was probably as good as you'd find outside of Ireland.

Andrew walked in well after dark without fanfare. The doorman welcomed him with a nod to say 'you're all set' and he walked into the bar, slowly taking in his surroundings. He was looking for familiar faces, mainly Bernadette's. 'Way too overzealous' he thought 'no way she'd be in this early.' Andrew smiled and waved to the bartender and pointed to the Guinness taps with his index finger. She nodded in understanding and mouthed 'I'll bring it over.'

Despite a solid layering of people at the bar, the tables were mainly empty. Andrew grabbed a small round table in the center of the bar with a clear view to both the television, which had the Bruins games on, and the front door. The bartender brought his Guinness over after a few minutes. When she placed it down Andrew thanked her quickly, then watched as the foam within the glass finally settled to a perfect black with a fully formed white head.

He sipped away slowly, wanting to pace himself to keep his wits intact. It was hard to do however as he sat alone flicking his eyes constantly in a pendulum swing from the Bruins game on TV to down at his dust covered smart phone, a new model that was already speckled white with drywall dust. 'What's the point in buying anything new' he thought as he attempted to rub away the debris from the screen.

During the third period of the game, finally a familiar face walked through the door. It wasn't Bernadette, not even close, but it was someone who might talk to him for a while and take his mind off the waiting. Chef Benson owned the convenient store on West Elm Avenue. Andrew had seen him get whacked in the head just that morning 'though it felt like weeks ago after the day I had' he thought. Chef walked in with his head on a swivel, by himself, quite obviously looking for beer and a chat. Andrew knew him growing up as Mike, but over the years he'd picked up the nickname 'Chef'. Andrew wasn't sure exactly where he got it, but expected its origin was as murky as it was random since to his knowledge, Mike Benson wasn't known for his prowess in the kitchen. He was just south of average in height, but kept in good shape. His hair was always neatly combed, and his face was always smiling. Andrew wasn't sure if it was part of his persona as a local business owner, or if he was just genuinely happy, but it made him easy to like all the same. Andrew knew him mostly just from the store, mainly just small talk or waving hello in the mornings, but they had hung out a few times over the years. Andrew made a point to keep his eyes up and be noticeable. He made eye contact with Chef followed by a wave as he walked further into the bar room.

Andrew nodded another hello and pointed with his open hand over to a chair at his table in a gesture that asked 'join me?' Chef nodded in the affirmative and headed towards the table, but not before dropping a ten dollar bill on the bar and placing an order. He walked over then, with a bottle of Bud light in this left hand. He held out his right to shake hands as he got closer and Andrew did the same. Close up, Andrew noticed a slight bruise on Chef's temple where he'd been clipped that very morning.

'How's it going Chef?' Andrew asked 'Hope you put some ice to that' he said and pointed to Chef's temple.

'Hey Dawson' Chef answered 'Yeah, well I threw a bag of peas on it for a while this morning. It's fine though, stunned me for a second that's all, but he didn't get me that good.'

'It looked like a clean enough connection. Well, from outside it did anyway.'

'Yeah, well it definitely did hurt at the time. Hey, by the way, thanks for trying to chase after the guy for me. I was calling out to you from the store. I didn't want you to go to the trouble.' Chef said.

'Don't worry about it' Andrew answered 'Sorry I let him get away.'

Chef shook his head 'No problem man. I didn't want

you to chase him cause I knew who it was anyway. Actually the cops picked him up later this morning.'

'No kidding? Who was it?' Andrew asked

'Actually a cousin of mine if you can believe it. Imagine that? Trying to rip off your own family like that?'

'No I can't actually' Andrew answered 'Sounds pretty low, sorry to say.'

'Yeah it was' Chef agreed 'Kid used to be alright, but he fell into hanging with the wrong crowd. I know that's what everyone says, but I feel like it's true for him. He got caught up with some of those dudes that hang around with John Bishop's crew. Have you heard of him? Bad dude by most accounts.'

Andrew shuttered with what could only be disgust at the mention of Bishop's name. 'Yeah, I know who he is' was all Andrew said.

'Well you know then.' Chef explained 'It's the same old story. My cousin started hanging around them, then next thing you know he's hooked on heroin and rolling over his cousin's convenient store for petty cash.'

Andrew nodded, 'Yeah, I know the type anyway.'

The bartender walked back over to the table again and put down another pint. She smiled and then backed away slowly. 'That from you?' Andrew asked Chef.

'Yeah man, cheers, least I could do after you tried to

help.'

'Cheers' Andrew said and raised his glass slightly in thanks. 'Not a big deal really.'

'Hope you don't mind man' Chef continued, 'I gave the cops your name when they showed up, just in case they needed a witness.'

'No problem. They know how to reach me?' Andrew asked

'Yeah I'm guessing they do. Hey speaking of which, why'd you guys take off so quick? The cops that showed up were hoping to talk to you on the spot. They waited for a while, but took off eventually.'

'Huh, yeah, it occurred to me actually.' Andrew said 'I guess when Stevie picked me up in my truck I just forgot and we headed off to work.'

'Stevie Black right?' Chef asked

'Yeah, you know him I'm sure, went to high school with us.'

'Yeah of course I do. He was kind of weird this morning actually, walked in real nonchalant, but very quick and got me to pour him a coffee. When I mentioned the cops were on their way, he just said that he figured as much, then paid and took off in your truck. I thought it was awkward. Kinda thought he'd pass the word to you to wait around.'

'Stevie can be like that sometimes. He's been on edge

lately for some reason. To be honest, I smelled booze off him when he picked me up, so maybe that's why he bounced, I don't know.'

Chef shrugged in reluctant agreement, seemingly not convinced. 'Yeah, could be I guess. So anyway, don't be surprised to hear from them at some point.'

'Whenever man. Whatever I can do.' He answered then thought to himself, 'Especially if it in some way impacts John Bishop. And definitely if it hurts him.'

John Bishop had a reputation in the neighborhood as someone to avoid at all costs. It was known that most of the drugs that found their way into Quincy and the surrounding area's streets passed through his hands first. The dirty money that accompanied it was cleaned through any number of local businesses that Bishop either owned or controlled. Andrew knew John Bishop well. He knew him better than probably anyone else. Unlike everyone else however, who whispered Bishop's name in either fear or reverence, anytime that name came across his lips he breathed it out with dragon fire.

Before the drugs, easy money, and reputation, John Bishop was just Johnny. He was a local kid who happened to be a best friend to Brian Dawson, Brian was Andrew's older brother. Bishop and Brian Dawson played in the same sandbox. They were friends since basically birth and remained best friends for a lifetime after that. Seven years his junior, Andrew spent much of his youth following behind or being bossed around by his brother Brian and by extension, John Bishop. Andrew went through his entire adolescence idolizing his brother and Bishop. He wanted to be like both of them in the worst way. He wanted to be noticed by them even more than that.

Hindsight is twenty-twenty, especially in this case. Whenever Andrew thought back to his early teen years and ran through those memories, he could spot the changes in Bishop like they appeared in slow motion. The rumors of Bishop's fist fights and other violent behavior became more and more frequent as Andrew reached high school. He could hear almost verbatim the words of warning accompanied by tears from his mother as she pleaded with her oldest son to break away from his friend. Andrew wasn't always clear on what she was upset about, but he felt the emotion in her tone even if her voice was muffled through walls and closed doors, not to mention the strengthening of her Irish accent that greatly intensified when she grew upset.

Eventually his brother did heed her advice to leave Bishop behind. Unfortunately he did so in a way that crushed his mother and brother greatly. He joined up. He enlisted in the military and within a year found himself on a

Navy battleship in the Persian Gulf during the Iraq war. By the time he left the Navy and returned home Andrew had grown into a man. At 17, he was a young man, but a man nonetheless. Unfortunately, also by that time, the rumors of drunkenness and fights involving John Bishop were replaced by whispers of drug connections, money, power and more extreme displays of violence. Much to Andrew and his mother's dismay, Brian Dawson and John Bishop's friendship lasted the distance a war put between them and upon his return, they were quick to reconnect.

The Bruins game ended just before ten o'clock with a one-goal game going in Boston's favor. Andrew was glad to have Chef Benson sit with him, even if they did just watch the game and not say much. When the final buzzer rang, Andrew shifted in his chair poised to run for the men's room since he'd been holding in a piss while waiting for a whistle. As he stepped off the stool he caught a breaking news announcement flash on the TV screen from the corner of his eye. The screen then showed two young, sun-kissed and well-dressed news anchors. It wasn't the plastic former beauty queen that caught Andrew's eye however, it was the news headline that rolled across the bottom of the screen. It read, 'missing Quincy woman found dead.'

'What happened there?' Andrew asked Chef Benson,

while pointing up at the TV screen. Chef turned towards the television. When he read the headline he shook his head sadly. 'That's terrible man. I can't believe she was found dead.'

'I hadn't heard anyone was missing' Andrew answered.

'Yeah, well, you hear a lot of news and gossip behind the counter of a neighborhood store.

'I guess so. Who was she anyway? Did you know her?' Andrew asked.

'Yeah man, shit you're way out of the loop. You know her too. It's Gina O'Neil, she graduated with us.'

Andrew's eyes widened in surprise. 'Fuck' he muttered. 'Yeah I knew her well actually.' His mind lingered back to a young girl he knew years ago. He thought of her short brown hair that used to curl inwards towards her face and partially cover cute dimples. 'She hung around with us a bit. I haven't seen her in a long time though. What's that make then, three girls in three years?'

'More like three girls found dead in less than two years I think. I don't know what the hell happened to this place. I don't remember it ever being that dangerous.'

'It can't be random though can it? I mean . . . that's way too big of a coincidence. For fucksake they all went to the same high school and all about the same age.' Andrew said.

'Tell me about it' Chef said, 'It's fucking sick, that's what it is.'

'I wonder if they have any suspects.'

Chef leaned in closer towards the middle of the table before replying. 'You see that dude over there?' Chef asked, and nodded with his eyes and a slight lift of his chin towards the corner of the bar closest to the front door.

Andrew had matched Chef's lean forward with one of his own, then shifted slowly to peer through a group of people standing at a table that blocked his view of the bar. He noticed a well-dressed black man in his mid-to-late thirties talking quietly with the bar's owner while slowly scanning the room. Andrew looked back at Chef, just missing eye contact with the man.

'The black dude? What . . . is he a suspect?'

Chef shook his head no. 'No man, he's the police. He's a homicide detective with the Staties.'

'He looks really familiar' Andrew said.

'Yeah, he should. He's from here. Pretty sure he was a running back at Quincy high in his day. I think he still helps out with some of the coaching.

'You seem to know a lot about him Chef.'

'He's a customer, so he's in the store a few times a week. It's part of the job to small talk. Like I said before, plenty of gossip, I do very little beyond shooting the shit all day in that place. After a while you get to know people, especially in this city. Everyone knows everyone around here.'

'Yeah I guess so.' Andrew agreed. 'Still, what's he doing here? He doesn't look like a regular, he's in too good shape to hang out at a bar.'

'Yeah, well, like I said, he's from the area. I imagine he knows the Mackins. Plus . . . maybe he has a suspect in mind.'

Andrew felt a shiver run up his spine when he realized what Chef was suggesting. 'You think he's looking for someone in here?' he asked.

'Hey, I don't know man' Chef answered 'I'm just speculating, probably same as everyone else. Only thing I know is three girls are gone in two years, all from the city of presidents?'

'Yeah, I guess so Chef. Still, it's creepy as fuck to think about it.'

'It is definitely. It's surreal alright, but I wouldn't be surprised to hear it's a local dude doing this. That's all I'm saying.'

CHAPTER FOUR

Andrew left Chef in Mackin's a short while later. He decided to leave his truck in the back behind the bar and walk home instead. The night actually grew warmer and more pleasant the later it got, the snow from that morning became a distant memory.

He walked steadily home, not rushing, but not strolling either. It was a good thirty minute walk back to his apartment, which was normally plenty of time to clear his head. Most nights it was, but not that night. He'd had a long day . . . a very long day. He was upset that Bernadette never showed up, but that drifted to the back of his mind for the moment, overshadowed by those three girls kidnapped and found dead. All were girls he knew pretty well in years past. 'God, even Gina O'Neil' he thought. 'He felt sad for her family, although he knew deep down, despite the sorrow, it meant very little to his day to day life. Gina had been a friend. In fact, there was a time he thought of her as a good friend, but that had long since passed and they were no longer in touch. He probably would've gone the remainder of his life without a single thought in her direction. He was pretty sure they weren't even Facebook friends. Maybe it was just human nature to be able to block out things that didn't impact your daily life. Perhaps it was some internal, instinctive defense mechanism allowing humans to wake up every day and keep moving forward despite all the shit that's wrong with the world. Logically it even made sense to let some things go in the background. Otherwise, each day there could be reasons to get upset. People could walk around with a permanent dread looming over them. That's not much of a life if that's the case. Most people want to just live their lives and be left the hell alone. 'If only it were that simple' Andrew thought 'If only the world and people in it had the capacity to live and let live. Unfortunately badness knows no bounds and the world has plenty of it, whether it's obvious or lays dormant in wait. It permeates mankind, taking host in every dark shadowed corner of the world. Look at the Catholic Church for fucksake' he thought, 'if only that were an extreme example, but it's really not.' Evil could be more subtle too, invisible much of the time only to rear its head at opportune moments through some influence or even mere suggestion.

Andrew felt it was this subtle, slow and deliberate evil

that chipped away at his brother until it eventually overcame him. He knew intellectually that his brother's downfall and death was not as black and white as he made it out to be. There were several factors and twists of fate at play. Instinctively though he blamed John Bishop. No one ever said pain and grief had to be rational. John Bishop was evil incarnate as far as Andrew was concerned. He was the lowest of the low, the personification of subtle badness. He was the driving force behind the current drug epidemic in the area. Surely if there was no Bishop, there'd be someone else driving it, there always is. But, there is a John Bishop, so in Andrew's eyes it's all on him. Andrew shook his head hoping to cast away his train of thought. Always, his mind went back to his brother Brian, and all dark roads in his head led to John Bishop.

'God, what happened to me?' he asked himself out loud as he walked. 'I swear I use to smile. I use to laugh even.'

He dug his hands into his pockets and picked up his pace as he turned a corner and headed up a steep hill that led to his apartment. 'It's been a long day that's all' he thought 'And Bernie didn't even show up. I'll be better tomorrow.'

His legs started to ache along with his back again as he climbed the hill towards his apartment. He made it to the side steps off the driveway. It was dark, near blackout on his porch, and it was quiet. The neighbors had all gone to bed, and the night was still except for the sound of water steadily dripping down the loose drain pipe that hung on its last remaining hinge. 'I'll have to mention that to the landlord before spring arrives and it keeps me up all night with the windows open.' He thought.

He reached the top step and the porch light came on suddenly and blinded him momentarily. Startled, he shifted quickly to his left dragging his right foot back to brace his weight. His vision cleared up quickly when his eyes adjusted to the light. He smiled at his intruder and settled his fighting stance down, bringing his hands back down to his sides with it.

'Something must have you on edge.' Bernadette said with a smile. 'I thought for a second you were going to attack me.'

'Jesus Christ Bernie,' he answered while letting out a breath he noticed he'd been holding. 'I very nearly did. You really know how to get a guy's heart rate up.'

'I try, thanks.' She said smiling.

'Don't thank me, I'll invoice you my medical bill. Shit you nearly gave me a heart attack.'

Andrew took a step back and looked Bernadette over. She had startled him and with good reason. 'Why was she here?' he thought. 'Of all places, she stakes out my porch. This is either really good or really bad.' Something instinctive told him it was more likely the latter.

She was dressed in skinny jeans with boots and a navy overcoat. She wore a hat as well, also navy, a cross between a beret and something a sailor might wear during the winter. Strands of her red hair crept out from under the hat and dangled fashionably around her face. Despite the rise in temperature, it was still brisk for the season, which showed on her flushed cheeks. 'She must've been here for quite some time' Andrew figured 'waiting in the cold for me. This doesn't feel right.'

After staring at her for what seemed an eternity, Andrew finally realized he hadn't asked her in. 'You must be cold' he said 'Do you want to come inside?'

Bernadette looked up, her blue eyes glistening in the moonlight. She slid over on the bench where she was sitting and motioned with her hand for him to join her. 'Let's sit out here for a while. It's nice out finally.'

Andrew shrugged slightly, then eased onto the bench next to her. She must have noticed his gingerly approach and gave him a look of concern. 'Your back still hurting you these days?' she asked.

'It's fine' Andrew answered 'Just tweaked it this morning again, that's all.'

'Maybe it's time to find a desk job ya think?' You'll be older than your years if you keep it up.'

'I don't see me lasting long or doing much good with a pencil or sitting behind a computer screen, but I get your point. Maybe I should've listened to my mother and went to college.'

'It's not too late for that Andrew. You know how many people go back to school these days? And I mean much older than you.'

'Maybe . . . probably not though. I still kick around joining up though. Maybe Army, maybe Navy.'

She gave him a disapproving look. 'Please Andrew, think long and hard about that choice.'

'I've thought of little else actually.' He answered. 'Give me a reason not to then. Give me a reason to stick around here.' He said almost pleading.

'Come on Andrew, you know I . . .' she hesitated. 'Your mother, she'd surely be upset, after, you know . . . your brother and everything.'

'Probably' Andrew agreed, clearly deflated by her response or lack thereof. 'Not that I see her now anyway.'

'That's right, sorry I forgot she moved back. Where is she now, still in Dublin?'

'No, not anymore she isn't. She moved home to Donegal.'

'Does she visit at all?' Bernadette asked

'She hasn't, no, but we Skype the odd time and really

that's all.'

Andrew's mother suffered a nervous breakdown the year his brother died. She'd been battling depression since forever. It grew noticeable after Andrew's father died when Andrew was twelve. She'd nearly come out of it, or at least seemed to emerge from the darkness briefly. But, when Andrew's brother Brian went to war, she couldn't cope with the stress of worrying about him. He survived the war alright, at least physically. Emotionally however, he was never the same. Next came the drinking. After that came the drugs. His mother's cries for help fell on deaf or tormented ears so they went unheeded for a long while. Heroin finally took him. The pressure of it all successfully took her. He died, she didn't. She did, however, melt. Living in America for thirty years was finally too much for her. She hopped on a plane to Dublin and stayed with relatives at first. After a while, she finally managed to move back to her family's home in a small town in Donegal. When the smoke cleared, Andrew found himself alone. Well, he had Bernadette then. And he had Stevie.

Andrew's mind drifted momentarily with the thought of his mother, but he quickly came back to the present. 'Enough' he thought, 'there's a reason she's here.'

'Bernie.' He said and shifted his body to face her directly. I spent the entire evening at Mackin's hoping for the chance to see you. After you didn't show, I resigned myself to that, only to come home and find you waiting for me on my porch. I need to know now. What are you doing here?'

'There, it's out there, on the line' he thought 'cards are on the table.'

He watched her stiffen slightly and noticed she looked nervous. She was biting down the corner of her lip. 'always when she's nervous' he thought and fear loomed over him.

He watched as she slowly, hesitantly pulled off her left glove with her right hand, finger by finger, one at a time. When it was off she held it towards him. He looked down at her hand, then up into her eyes which now shone with the beginning of tears.

'Does that mean what I think it means?' he asked while trying to swallow the lump in his throat.

'It does Andrew. I'm getting married.' She answered.

Andrew leaned back against the bench and brought his hands up to his head and locked his fingers behind it. He let out a slow breath. He said nothing. She noticed.

'I had to tell you in person Andrew, that's why I'm here. I. . .'

'It's okay' he said and slowly stood up, putting his hand up in a gesture to stop her from elaborating.

'You're leaving?' she asked, clearly hurt.

'I want to happy for you Bernie . . . it's just . . . I need time.'

She stood up and put her glove back on quickly. 'I'm sorry if I hurt you Andrew. It's just not something I could've lived with telling you over the phone or having you find out any other way. I'm going now.'

She reached over and hugged him, then kissed him on the cheek. Andrew stood frozen like a statue, thinking for a second that her touch, her final touch, had turned him to stone. In a way, he'd guessed that it actually had. He watched her get to her car and drive off safely. His mind raced. He let himself into the apartment and double-locked the door behind him then planted himself face first down onto his couch. After a minute, sleep finally took him.

CHAPTER FIVE

The next morning came quickly for Andrew. He woke up right where he laid down the night before. His body ached with a night of uncomfortable sleep on a sofa not big enough to hold a man of his size lying horizontal for that length of time. He stood up and stretched grazing his fingertips at full reach against the ceiling. His clothes felt too loose on his body after being slept in. He threw on running pants and a sweatshirt and headed for the kitchen. He chased down the last of his ibuprofen with some orange juice and threw a bagel in the toaster. Waiting for it to pop, he dialed Stevie's cell phone number. Stevie picked up after four rings sounding groggy, but awake.

'Any luck last night?' he asked.

'Only bad luck actually. Let me wake up a bit and I'll walk you through it later.' Andrew answered, then asked, 'We're on for today right?'

'Yeah fuck it, might as well, we ain't working.'

'Good, I need to burn off some beers, not to mention blow off steam.'

'Outside the store in an hour? I have to go get my truck first.'

'Sounds perfect, I'll get my gear ready.'

'Later Stevie.' He said then hung up. Any weekend that Andrew and Stevie didn't work was used for training. Over the years between the two of them they had done some boxing, kung fu, jiu jitsu, even Krav Maga. Through a little experience and a lot of drive, they jointly put together a series of different workouts incorporating things each had learned over the years, both in relation to self-defense and general working out. A lot of what they did involved running, sometimes calisthenics, but all involved some form of hand to hand fight training or weapons defense.

Each had gone through his coming of age fist fights, but this wasn't really about that. It was more about preparation. Preparation for what, Andrew could never figure out, but for one reason or another he always carried a niggling dread that his days of physical altercation were not over. Maybe it was the stress of physical labor and working in close quarters with other stressed out men on different building sites. Maybe it had something to do with his past, his father dying on foot of a road rage incident or watching his brother go off to war. 'Or maybe, it was just too much fucking television.' He thought. Regardless of the driving force, like everything else, after years of doing it, it became somewhat of a custom. It was never for show and never something either Andrew or Stevie talked about to others. It was just something they did together. Like going to the gym, it was part of their normal routine.

Andrew pulled into his usual spot in the shop's front parking lot. He looked around after he put the truck in park, but didn't see any sign of Stevie yet. 'No surprise there' He thought.

He entered the shop through the front, nodding to the teenager behind the counter, while he headed towards the back for the large refrigerator. He grabbed a gallon of water and two large Gatorades from the fridge. He walked to the front of the small shop and put the items on the counter. 'I thought Chef opened up every morning?' he asked the young man. 'He does usually' the man answered. 'He texted me last night to see if I'd cover for him on the early shift. I work it sometimes, usually the mornings after he's been out on the sauce.'

'He must trust you, that's good.'

'Yeah, I guess so. Brothers can be like that.'

'Oh, sorry I didn't realize Chef had a brother. I'm Andrew.'

'He does and I'm him. I know who you are, you're friends with that dude Stevie right?'

'Yes, I am.' Andrew answered. 'How do you know Stevie?'

'Just from around' He answered, 'plus he comes in here a lot. He's kind of a dick if you don't mind me saying. He's always calling me Sous chef.'

Andrew smiled and laughed briefly. 'Yeah, I guess he can be. What's your real name?'

'It's David'

'Okay David, good talking to you.' He said and handed over a five dollar bill for the drinks. He grabbed the bottles between his knuckles and lifted the gallon with his free hand and backed through the door on his way out, nodding good bye as the door chimed behind him.

'Top of the morning bud' Stevie yelled from over next to the passenger door as Andrew walked down the steps.

'What's up Stevie' Andrew answered.

'One of those for me?' Stevie asked pointing to the Gatorade.

'Yup' Andrew said and stuck one bottle under his armpit and under-handed the other to his friend. He reached over the bed of the truck and put the gallon of water into the back. When he did, he saw Stevie's old North Quincy High School hockey bag lying next to it. 'You brought some

53

props I take it?'

'Of course. I got a few new things in there to try out.'

Andrew opened the driver's door and stepped up into the truck, he reached over and flung the passenger door open from the inside. Stevie climbed in and stuck his Gatorade in the center cup holder.

'What'd you bring this time?' Andrew asked.

'Not much new really. Brought wooden short swords and knives, some markers . . . oh and a couple of real blades I picked up recently.'

'Real blades huh?'

'You know, for authenticity.' Stevie answered and smiled.

Every time they went training, Stevie stuffed his old hockey bag with weapons, some real, some fake. Mostly what they practiced with were wooden replicas of weapons that Stevie spent time fashioning himself. That way, the motions were true to life and they could go full force without really killing each other. The markers were a poor substitute for weapons, because the size and shape were all wrong. But, they were a good way to decide who won the fight. He with the least purple swipes of Crayola was generally deemed the winner, unless the other came away with a strip across the neck or something similar.

Most of what they practiced was hand to hand combat.

They used padded gloves a lot. Other than that, they practiced a hell of a lot on knife disarms. Stevie also sanded down a set of wooden pistols to practice gun disarms, but realistically unless you were within arms-length or closer to someone pointing a gun, conventional wisdom was to run like hell and scream.

Andrew hated knives and felt sick at the thought of what blades did to human flesh. He feared them. He feared guns too, but felt like knives were easier to access and therefore more likely to come across. Although the ease and likelihood gap between knives and guns grew more narrow each day. Still, it was knife fighting, particularly, learning to disarm someone wielding one that he worked hardest to perfect.

There was one disarm in particular he and Stevie referred to as "the move". The move was what they practiced most. Andrew could pull it off in his sleep. Stevie however was very much against it as a viable technique. This was for a few reasons. Firstly, it wasn't something either of them were taught by a trained martial arts or self-defense coach. In fact, they saw it first in a low budget Steven Segal movie before either of them entered puberty. They had been practicing it since then. The other reason Stevie spoke against the move was because in order to pull it off, the attacker's arm would have to strike with the knife straight forward at about neck level or higher. Stevie always said that it was more likely that an attacker stab low and straight or slash with a high swipe. He argued vigorously and often against anyone knowingly trying to stab someone in the bony chin. Nevertheless, it looked bad ass when Segal did it and they worked on it since they were young, so they stuck with it out of habit.

The move itself was simple on paper. It was much more difficult in practice. When an attacker struck out straight forward so that his arm is elevated at the victim's height or higher, the intended victim bounces back from his lead foot, tilting his head to the outside and sweeping the knife hand in the opposite direction. Next, his strong hand tightly clutches the attacker's knife wielding wrist and he pivots the lead foot bringing the weak side shoulder upwards hard into the attacker's elbow. The aim is to break the elbow, not just hyper extend it, so force is key. The last part is circumstantial and fortuitous at best, but what should happen is that the elbow break and corresponding shriek of pain should free the knife. It should at least loosen it, making it possible to grab with the strong hand, pivot with the back foot and plunge the knife straight forward into the attacker's own heart.

Andrew agreed it was unlikely to ever be useful, but felt at least it was an exercise in coordination and speed. Plus, he was a sucker for nostalgia.

A short drive later and Andrew and Stevie pulled into Marina Bay. Marina Bay is a plot of water front land on Dorchester Bay overlooking Boston's city skyline seven miles to the north. Years of development and an influx of cash turned it into a hot waterfront town, with Condo's, bars and restaurants, night clubs and office buildings. Like any old beach town however, it was virtually dead during winter months and severely overcrowded in the summer. With winter dragging on into March, the place gave off a desolate air.

Andrew weaved his truck through the newly minted roads and drove into the large parking lot towards the back of the marina. He parked at the very end of the lot where cement and concrete gave way to dirt and wild brush before the uninhabited section of the property. He killed the ignition and helped Stevie grab the bag from the back of the truck. They began walking down a dirt path, towards the bay about a mile in the distance. They had discovered this semi-secluded beach back in high school. A few times they had been to small parties on the beach. Eventually however the local police caught on to the underage drinking taking place and put a stop to the festivities. That was years ago. Since then the small hidden sand patch overlooking the city remained untouched. They started working out there around the same time Stevie started bringing out more and more obviously dangerous weapons to practice with. When that happened, co-users of the local baseball fields were no longer so welcoming. Apparently playgrounds and martial arts weaponry were not a great mix.

The walk down the dirt path was more or less silent. Having been friends for so long and still spending plenty of time together meant that periods of silence or long pauses in conversations were not awkward. In fact, they were often a nice break from arguing with each other.

Stevie stepped forward and ducked his head under a low hanging branch to enter the grounds of the beach. Andrew followed behind him. The sand was dark and tightly packed with moisture. The small surf had left branches and other debris where the water met the sand. The morning still had a dull edge, but the sky was bright despite the cloud cover.

'So, you ready to talk yet?' Stevie asked as he hoisted the bag onto a small dune protected by a large rock. 'You haven't said shit about last night.'

Andrew had already begun stretching out and answered Stevie as he pulled his arm across his body and twisted his waist. 'She's getting married I guess. That's pretty much all there is to say.'

Stevie pushed out his bottom lip and nodded his head slowly several times. 'So she's gonna settle for that douche bag she's been going out with?'

'Apparently, yes. I don't know why I'm surprised. I guess . . . just some part of me always felt we'd end up together, you know.'

'What a bitch.' Stevie said.

'Dude, come on I'm not sure I'm ready to bad mouth her. It's her decision really. It's not like we were going out.'

'Yeah, well, you're a faggot then. Let her marry some fucking accountant from Pennsylvania, what do I care?'

'He probably isn't a bad guy. I'm pretty sure of that actually.' Andrew replied.

'Dude, I've seen him before.' Stevie said shaking his head. 'He wears Dockers and clips his fucking cell phone to his belt.'

Andrew just shrugged. 'Alright . . . maybe he does sound like a douche bag.'

'Yeah, and that d bag is banging your girl.'

'Real nice.' Andrew said.

'Just speaking the truth my man, and you know it.' Stevie said and dropped to a knee to tie his sneakers.

'Hey, did you hear about Gina O'Neil?' Andrew asked.

Stevie finished tying his lace and stood back up. 'Yeah, I did actually. Too bad.'

'Yeah, to say the least.'

'I heard they found her body under the Neponset bridge.'

'Really? Well . . . maybe she was dumped there.'

'I wouldn't think so.' Stevie said.

'Why not? '

'Place is swimming with cops, that's why. They always park under the bridge. Probably just to prevent that shit from happening outside the hotel beside there ya know, and other stuff like drug deals and shit. She was probably dumped upstream and the current took her.'

'I guess. You appear to be the expert.'

'No expert buddy, just logic. Anyway here, let's get started before I decide to go back to bed.' Stevie said, then took off in a sprint across the small beach. Andrew, a few steps behind, followed after.

They ran a few laps, then rested, then ran a few more. Once the heart rate was up, they hit some stretches, then straight into rounds with the gloves and pads. Once it got to a point where Andrew felt his arms would fall off, he asked 'Want to switch it up?' To answer his own question, he tore the Velcro strap from the outside of his glove with his teeth and pulled off the mitt using his arm pit for leverage.

Stevie threw the pads down and crouched down to look into the hockey bag. He rummaged through it for a few seconds, then pulled out something about the size of a wooden serving spoon that was wrapped in a cloth. He lobbed it underhanded to Andrew. 'Here' he said.

Andrew caught the object in both hands and carefully unwrapped the towel around it. Inside was a knife with a polished wooden handle and a long blade with small serrated peaks that thinned to a sharp point at the top. 'It looks like a steak knife on steroids.' Andrew said.

He gripped the handle with his right hand and carefully held the blade across the palm of his left. 'It definitely doesn't look legal.' He scraped his thumbnail across the knife edge in the way a hockey player checks his skates for sharpness. Unconvinced, he put his finger tip on the top of the knife, which cut it immediately drawing blood from his finger, which dripped down the blade. 'Fuck!' he said and shook his hand loose then brought the fingertip to his mouth. 'It's wicked sharp, thanks for the warning.'

'It's a knife Andrew, what'd you expect?' Stevie answered. Andrew smiled and nodded. 'Where'd you find it anyway?' he asked. 'You know I've been trying to pick up some side work? Anyway, I was helping this guy Mike Doyle sheetrock his basement. When we were clearing it out, he gave it to me along with a set of old golf clubs.'

'Not bad' Andrew said and nodded. 'Hope he paid you with more than just his old shit.' Andrew dropped it back into the towel and got up to put it back in the bag. He picked up a wooden knife instead. 'I'm not practicing with that thing. Here get up, we'll use the wooden fakes.'

'Pussy' Stevie answered and smiled as he jumped back to his feet.

'Yeah okay, whatever, a pussy cause I don't want to gut my best friend like a fish.' He stepped towards the clearing, then quickly started swiping at Stevie with the wooden blade.

CHAPTER SIX

They worked out for over an hour before calling it quits. Both dripped with sweat as the spring sun arrived at last and burnt off the early cloud cover with it. Andrew carried the bag back to the truck and flung it over the side when they reached it. He put his hands out and grasped the side of the truck bed then squatted down as far as he could. He felt his lower back stretching and it felt good, a vast improvement from the days before. 'Want me to drop you back home?' he asked Stevie.

'No actually. But can you swing me by Wollaston train station? I need to run into Dee Dee's.' Andrew slowly stood up and leaned over the truck bed to look at his friend. He paused before responding, confused because Dee Dee's lounge was a small dive bar across the street from the train station. No one really went there, except for John Bishop's crew. Rumor was Bishop acquired it at some stage. It was a debt payoff. He kept it open so he could conduct business in a legitimate establishment. 'Yeah, sure I'll drop you there.' Andrew answered 'but that's Bishop's place.'

'I know who's place it is Andrew.'

'So, you're in with Bishop now?'

'What? Come on man. Of course I'm not working for Bishop. I just know some of his people. That guy Doyle I mentioned. He's apparently one of Bishop's crew . . . I didn't know that when I took the job Andrew, I swear.'

'Fine' Andrew said and opened the door and got into the truck. Stevie followed suit on the passenger side. 'You don't need to come in or anything. Plus I heard that Bishop's hardly ever there, so you won't run into him.'

'You think I'm scared of Bishop?' Andrew asked

'Aren't you?'

'Please.' Andrew said.

'No.' Stevie said and laughed, 'You're not scared of Bishop. I saw you bounce him off of every car on Kingston Street. But . . . you are scared of trouble.'

'Fuck you Stevie. I'll drop you off there, don't worry. You can stop selling it to me.'

'Thanks Andrew. Ya know . . . you're my hero.'

'Prick' Andrew said. He fought to hold back a smile, then started the truck and pulled away.

The drive to the train station was silent from that point

onwards. Andrew drove the truck around the back of Wollaston train station's parking lot to avoid the main street's traffic. He pulled up close to the curb and Stevie jumped out. Each managed a 'see ya later' before Stevie slammed the door and headed down the steps to the station's swinging doors.

Andrew's cell phone started ringing while he was still sitting idle. He looked at the screen. The number was local, but he didn't recognize it since it wasn't programmed into his phone. 'Hello' he answered.

A man's voice said 'Hi, Andrew?'

'Yeah it is' Andrew answered

'Hey man, it's Chef Benson. Is this a good time?'

'Ah, yeah, hey Chef, what's going on?'

'Remember I mentioned that those cops might need to talk to you? Well they were here again today and wanted to see if you could drop into the police station and give an official statement.'

'Oh. Okay, I didn't realize I'd have to go to them.'

'Yeah, sorry man, I didn't either, my bad.'

'Nah, don't worry about it Chef, I can do it today no problem, I'm not working.'

'Thanks Andrew, I appreciate it.'

'No problem, anything to help man.'

Andrew hit end on the cell phone and dropped it into

the center console. He put the truck into drive and pulled away from the curb slowly, joining traffic just before the intersection. It was mildly irritating that the cops needed him to go into the station for a statement, but he had told Chef he'd do whatever he could to help, so he felt obligated.

He arrived at the police headquarters quickly. The building sat on a corner overlooking the YMCA and a baseball field on the left and a cemetery to the right. He drove into the parking lot next to the building which was manned by one officer and had a gate as a barrier. Andrew rolled down the window and spoke to the officer. 'Hi, I was asked to come in and give a statement. Do I need to sign in or anything?'

'No' he yelled from the hut 'just park over next to the building and give your information to the officer at the front desk.'

'Thanks' Andrew said and waved. He continued into the parking lot and parked at a spot against the building as instructed. He walked around the building to the front entrance. Inside it was dark and appeared dusty like someone just shook out a carpet. A large metal door closed off the public to the rest of the department. The remainder of the room was plexi-glassed. Andrew noticed a female officer sitting behind the glass. He waved and smiled. She gave him the 'one minute' sign with her finger.

Andrew looked around while he waited. There wasn't much else to the room, just some official forms slotted next to a bulletin board that held posters for several hotline numbers. He felt self-conscious suddenly, and put on his best nonchalant stance. He had that irrationally guilty feeling like the one that arrives when approaching the passport control counter.

He heard the window slide open and turned towards it. 'Good morning' the policewoman said. Andrew stepped over towards the window and answered. 'Hi. Good morning. I'm here to give a statement.'

'Okay, do you know the detective in charge of the case?'

'I don't actually. It's related to a robbery I witnessed in a store. West Elm variety. It's a convenience store near Wollaston beach.'

'Okay' she answered, 'I can take your statement, I'm familiar with the case. Detective Maloney's in charge of that one and he's not in. Just give me a minute.'

She then shut the window and disappeared into the back.

A minute later another officer sat at the window and at the same time, the large metal door opened and the police woman waved Andrew in. He followed her through the door and eventually into a room that was furnished with a table and four folding chairs. 'Have a seat' she said as she shut the door then took a seat herself. 'I'm Officer

Donovan.'

Andrew looked at her. He recognized her. 'I'm Andrew Dawson. I think we were in high school together.' He said. 'You were a few years ahead of me.'

'You're right. Sorry, I did recognize you, but couldn't place you until now. You had a brother . . . Brian, right?'

'Yes. I did.' Andrew answered.

'So, anyway, your statement . . . why don't you walk me through what happened first, then I'll have you write it down and we'll sign it. That sound okay?'

'Um, yeah.' Andrew said 'That's fine with me.'

He gave her a play by play breakdown of what he saw. She asked some questions to help him remember details and also that helped him filter out anything he might have inferred but hadn't actually seen. The whole process took under an hour. When he finished, he wrote out the statement verbatim, then she read it aloud back to him. Next each signed the bottom of the form.

'Thanks for coming in' she said as she led him out through the hall. I'll walk you out.'

He followed her down the same path she had led him in and back through the heavy door into the waiting area. 'Here, I'll walk you outside to make sure the officer at the gate sees that we're done and you're good to go.'

Andrew left the building and held the door for her. 'How

long have you been a cop?' he asked.

'I've been on the force for over three years now.'

'You like it?'

'I love it actually.'

Andrew nodded, 'That's great. Wish I did something I loved.'

'What are you up to these days?'

'I'm a carpenter. I do mostly residential work now, like putting windows in and hanging vinyl siding.'

'That doesn't sound so bad.'

'Yeah, I know. It's not bad really. It's just not something I jump out of bed for every morning. I guess I'm lucky to have work these last few years.'

'I hear you, there are plenty of people without it, that's for sure.'

'Anyway, here's my truck.' Andrew said and slapped the bed of his Ford. He looked up at her and noticed she was looking into the back of his truck.

'Ah, hey Andrew? What do you have in the back here?' She asked.

Andrew followed her gaze to the open hockey bag with assorted weaponry in full view. 'Oh, shit' he thought. 'I forgot Stevie left the bag with me.' He paused, not sure what to say. He felt . . . indefensible and dumb as shit.

Finally, he spoke up, 'Those are . . . well, they're weapons actually. Mostly knives, swords and clubs, but it's not what it looks like.'

'Oh yeah? Tell me what it looks like?'

'I guess it looks like a bag of weapons.'

'And is it a bag of weapons?'

'Well, yes.'

'So it sounds like it's exactly how it looks.'

'Yeah' he said 'I guess it does. They're for training . . . martial arts training.'

'Andrew?'

'Yes?'

'I figured as much, but honestly, I can't let you drive out of here with those.'

'Okay' he answered 'I understand. Am I in trouble here?'

'Honestly, I don't think so, but I'll need to take them for now. I should actually take you in . . . but, listen let me take the bag. I need to speak with my sergeant.'

Andrew just waited. He was afraid to move. He kept away from the driver's door and kept his hands visible just in case. He watched Officer Donovan as she stepped backwards a few feet away, out of earshot, but kept her eyes up. She was alert to head off any sudden movement, which Andrew had no plans to make. He watched her lips moving as she spoke into the radio near her shoulder, then held it near her ear as she listened for the response while nodding.

Andrew couldn't tell what that nodding meant for his fate. She walked back over finally.

'I need to take the bag for now Andrew. Considering you came in on your own accord, you're free to go. We'll need to inspect what you have here. Anything that may be illegal will likely be confiscated, but you should get the rest back.

'Okay, I understand.' He said. Andrew watched her reach over and carefully haul the bag over the truck bed. She laid it on the ground at her feet, then waved at the officer guarding the gate.

'We'll call you and let you know what you can pick up. Bye for now Andrew.'

'Officer Donovan' he yelled.

'Yes?'

'Um . . . thank you.'

She waved again, a hesitant goodbye. Andrew let out a deep breath he'd been holding. He fired up the Ford and when the barrier lifted he drove out slowly, fighting the urge to peel out. 'Idiot' he thought as he took a left towards the beach.

CHAPTER SEVEN

Stevie's cell phone kept going direct to voicemail. Andrew dialed it three times in the span of twenty minutes. He drove back to Dee Dee's lounge in Wollaston and parked on a side street looking towards the bar on the corner facing the train station across the street. He debated whether he should just walk in, but he wanted to avoid any trouble if it was possible. He turned the ignition key backwards to let the radio play lightly without burning through a tank of gas. He was angry at himself for getting Stevie's stuff confiscated, but he found himself strangely calm and relaxed sitting in his truck watching the cars breeze past on the busy street in front of him. He watched as people entered and exited the train station. He noticed mostly young people, probably early twenties going in, and mainly workers, carpenters likely or laborers, coming out. He imagined the tradeoff was the young ones heading into Boston to party, while the working men made their way home after a short shift on Saturday at the building site. The former looking spritely and energetic, the latter looking weary yet satisfied with the opportunity to work an extra shift.

He lost himself people watching, and before he realized thirty minutes had passed. 'I'll try him one last time' he thought, and picked up his phone from the console. He ran his thumb across the screen to open his recent calls. He tapped Stevie's name to start the call. He put the phone to his ear in time to hear the start of the voicemail greeting. He didn't bother with a message, just hit call end on the screen and tossed the phone into the passenger seat. He peered across at the bar and noticed the door swing slowly open. Two men walked out. One was Stevie, still wearing a zipper up hoodie with his hands dug into the front pockets. The other man walked out behind him with a cigarette in his mouth. He used both hands to light it, blocking the flame from a slight breeze from the passing cars. Andrew recognized him as one of Bishop's guys, but he wasn't sure of his name.

He felt awkward suddenly as it dawned on him that he was spying on his best friend. He considered whether he could pull away without being noticed. He slid down an inch or two to hide his face behind the steering wheel, knowing full well it was pointless since Stevie knew his truck. As he thought it, Stevie happened to look over in his direction. He appeared to pause his conversation as he stepped forward towards the curb and crouched slightly to peer over with a hand up to shield the glare.

'Caught' Andrew thought. He waved and Stevie stood straight again and returned the wave. Andrew had no choice but to join them. He took his keys from the ignition and jumped down from the truck. He brushed the wrinkles from his shirt as he walked towards the two men. He cut across the street in front of a couple of cars stopped at a red light.

'Andrew' Stevie said and nodded.

'Hey Stevie' Andrew answered. 'Figured you'd still be here.'

'Yeah, I am. This is Mike Doyle?' he said pointing to the other man. The man pulled the cigarette from his mouth with his left hand and stretched out his right. Andrew took a slow step towards the man and shook his hand briefly.

'I'm Andrew.'

'How's it going? You look familiar. I've seen you around I think.'

'Likewise' Andrew said. He turned back towards Stevie. 'Hey, can I talk to you for a minute?'

Mike Doyle took a drag from his cigarette and flicked it into the street. 'I'm heading inside anyways.' He turned and walked back into the bar room.

The doors swung open and closed behind him. Andrew couldn't help but think of an old western movie. He caught a glimpse of inside the barroom when the door opened. It was dark. The only light seemingly from the Budweiser sign lit up behind the bar. He saw at least three others inside including the bartender. He recognized none of them.

He turned back towards Stevie now that his friend was out of ear shot. 'Hey man.' He said.

'Hey. Weird, you showing up here, waiting out front like some pervert watching a playground from a distance.'

'Yeah. Sorry. I called a few times. I didn't really want to barge in there you know.'

'Yeah okay.' He said. 'What's the emergency anyway?'

'There's no emergency. I just wanted to give you a heads up. I went to the police station to give a statement to the cops for Chef Benson. When I was leaving, the cop noticed the bag of weapons in the back of the truck. She made me leave them with her. I don't know what I'll be able to get back. I got the vibe they're gonna confiscate most of it.'

Andrew looked up at Stevie. He read irritation on Stevie's face, but he didn't say anything for a few seconds. 'Anyway. I just wanted to let you know, in case you were looking for them.'

'Fuck.' Stevie said after a moment. His eyes went bright and distant at the same time. He looked to be considering something internally. After a few seconds, he looked back at Andrew, smiled and shrugged. 'That sucks . . . okay, well, don't worry about it. It's not the end of the world.' He said. 'Did you let them know it was my bag?' he asked.

Andrew shook his head no. 'Nah, didn't occur to me.' He said. 'She assumed it was mine I'm guessing, no reason not to.'

Stevie stepped back and stood up straight. He looked up the street at nothing in particular. When he looked back at Andrew, he said 'Alright . . . let me get back in there. I need to finish up with this guy Doyle. I assume you don't want to come in.'

'No, I'm all set. Like I said, I just wanted to give you a heads up. I'll catch up with you later.'

Andrew turned to walk back to his truck. As he started across the street he heard the swinging bar doors creak behind him.

'Hey!' he heard someone yell out. He turned to see Mike Doyle walking back out towards him. 'I do know you don't I? You're Dawson's brother. I've heard about you.'

Andrew paused in the street. He shrugged then turned to Stevie silently requesting an intervention. Stevie must have understood the look because he cut in front of Doyle and began to corral him back inside.

'Later Andrew' He said and held his hand up in a wave.

Andrew answered 'see ya later Stevie' and continued back to his Ford.

CHAPTER EIGHT

Andrew's Saturday night consisted of pizza and beers by himself in front of the television. As punishment for his indulgence he headed out Sunday morning for a long run. He ran through Quincy's Wollaston and Montclair neighborhoods and continued north for a couple miles until he reached Dorchester. Then he turned and ran back on the same route. He kicked himself as he struggled up the several hills on the return path.

A shower and shave later he found himself bored and lonely in his apartment. Shortly thereafter, he found himself behind a piece of electrical tape on the floor of Mackin's Saloon. The tape on the ground marked the legal distance from the dartboard. Andrew stood behind the marker and repeatedly threw darts at the board. He threw six darts, walked to the board, pulled them out, and repeated. He wasn't alone in the bar. There were two men sitting at the bar trading complaints and a table of women in the corner drinking wine. The women looked like the after church crowd and were at odds with the bar's surroundings.

Andrew chatted periodically with the lone bartender in between throws, but he seemed too preoccupied with cleaning behind the bar and sweeping floors for idle chit chat. 'For what' Andrew thought. 'This place will be lucky to see fifteen people between now and Thursday.' He held the weight of the three darts remaining in his hand. He quickly fired the last three one at a time at the board, harder than was necessary.

'You mad at something?' a female voice said behind him.

He scrunched his eyebrows at the question and turned around slowly, surprised to see Bernadette standing less than two feet behind him. He smiled at her. She smiled back.

'Honestly, we need to get you a bell or something.' He said.

'I'm stealthy huh?'

'You're ninja-esque alright. What brings you here? Last I checked you weren't a Sunday drinker.'

'Look who's talking. Come on Andrew, it's not even football season.'

He laughed. 'You sound worried about me.'

'Maybe a little bit.' She said.

'Is that why you're here?'

'It's not the ambiance.'

'Seriously.'

'Seriously. I wanted to see if you were still mad. Considering how hard you threw the last few darts, I'd say yes, you are.'

'Oh that . . . No, I'm more accurate when I throw fast.'

She looked at the dart board. Six darts were stuck in the board, but none were remotely close to the center. 'Really?' she asked.

He shrugged his shoulders. 'They're not stuck in the wall right?'

'True I guess.' So which is it? Mad?'

He bit his lip and took a few seconds to respond. 'I can't stay mad at you. Let's call it disappointed.'

'Very parental thing to say.'

'I was thinking more school teacher, maybe principal. But you get it.'

Well. Do you want to talk for real?'

'I didn't realize we weren't.'

'Come on Andrew.'

'Okay. But . . . you know, what's it been, a day? I think I need some more time to deal with it before . . .'

'Before what?'

'You know, before we can be friends I guess.'

She bit her lip now and looked like she had more to say, but she just answered with 'I know you do. Well, I just wanted to see you before I headed back to Boxford. I'm on my way now.'

'Back to the cows?'

'Yup, and the deer . . . and don't forget the pigs. So, I'll see you when I see you?'

'Sure. See you when I see you.' He answered.

She smiled back and turned to walk out the side door of the bar. Before she left, Andrew yelled over to her, 'Bernie!'

'Yeah' she answered

'Congratulations. Really. I am happy for you.'

'Thanks Andrew.' She waved again then stepped out the door.

'See you' he said to himself finally after she walked out.

CHAPTER NINE

The body and mind are amazing tool sets. Many things they accomplish are done without having conscious knowledge of it. A loud bang can cause the heart to beat quickly sending blood flowing rapidly to limbs preparing the body for fight or flight. The unconscious mind spots problems or errors before the brain can put meaning or words to it. Using data gathered by all available senses, the brain compiles an assessment of a situation and sends the body into action, while conscious understanding of those actions arrives much later, as an afterthought really.

So, before Andrew knew why he was running, his legs were pumping like pistons. As he ran, his mind began to catch up and put pieces of information together. He woke up late for work on Monday, which meant he was late to the store to pick up Stevie. He parked his truck and climbed out, planning to pick up a coffee in the store. He noticed then that two very similar blue sedans were parked equidistant from the shop's entrance. Despite being late there was no sign of Stevie waiting in the parking lot. The lot itself was empty. As he stood there, he saw Chef Benson through the window. Chef was always smiling. He smiled when he sneezed. He probably smiled in his sleep too. But this morning, Chef was not smiling. He pictured Chef's face and the slight turn of his head when they made eye contact. He knew then that something was wrong. So, he ran. He didn't think about it really at the time. He didn't consider whether he had any reason to take off. He just set off in a sprint down the street towards the beach.

He didn't stop at the beach. He turned left at the corner and continued north running down Quincy Shore Drive. It was early morning, but there were plenty of cars on the road. A grown man running in work boots and jeans must've looked awkward. Had he time to look, he would have noticed plenty of double takes and lingering looks from commuters driving by.

As he reached the main intersection, he felt his lungs beginning to burn and his legs grew weary, no doubt due to his heavy boots and the initial adrenaline wearing off. He slowed to a jog at the corner, pausing only to gauge his timing before running across the street. He saw the Dunkin Donuts in front of him and headed for it, hoping to melt into the crowd. He needed to catch his breath and more importantly, he needed to think for a minute. He reacted. He wasn't sure what was actually happening. Chances were, he thought, 'no one's even chasing after me.'

He slid past a series of customers that were on their way out of the coffee shop. The place was full, which was typical on any weekday morning. Andrew walked to the back and took one of the few small tables. There was debris still on the table from the previous inhabitants, but at least it looked like he bought something. He put the palms of his hands up to his face and rubbed his eyes.

He tried to piece together in his head what he knew, or really, what he believed based on what he saw. The convenience store was definitely surrounded by cops. The two cars on either side were unmistakably cop cars. No one drives navy blue Crown Victoria's. At least very few did. That made it unlikely to have two randomly parked so close together. Then there was Chef's demeanor. He could see it from the street. Chef wasn't being Chef, no smile, no animation in his movements. He was stiff. He looked nervous. Then there was the look he gave Andrew through the glass. It was strange. Andrew interpreted it as a warning. There was no sign of Stevie, but that alone could be coincidence. It was Monday morning after all. What Andrew couldn't figure was, 'Why the need for a setup?'

'Why stage a pickup like that? Was it just over some

small weapons that he willingly turned over? They were more like props than anything. Then again' he thought, 'why would I run for that?' His nerves began to kick in. 'How must that look? Why would I take off like that? It had to have been fear, but would anyone buy that? I surely look guilty of something now.'

A voice spoke from across the table and broke Andrew's train of thought. He hadn't heard what the voice said, just registered the noise and felt the shadow of someone standing over him. As the man stood, he blocked out the sunlight from the window. Andrew looked up and acknowledged him. 'Excuse me?' he asked.

'I asked if this seat was taken.' the man said.

'No, go ahead.' Andrew answered.

The man pulled out the chair and sat down across from Andrew. He left the chair out a little from the table so he could cross a leg over his knee.

Andrew watched him dig into his inside pocket. When he pulled his hand out, a leather wallet came with it. He flipped it open to reveal a police badge. It was then that Andrew recognized the man from Mackin's Saloon. He was the state police detective that Chef pointed out a few nights ago.

'Do you know who I am?' the man asked.

'Ah . . . not by name. You're obviously a cop.'

'That I am son. I'm Detective Harris with the state police. And you're Andrew Dawson.'

'Yes sir I am.'

'Have a nice jog?'

'Not really, no.'

'Do you often take off on morning sprints?'

'No sir. I . . . got spooked I guess.'

'Okay, well, you're here now. There's a few ways we can go about this. The easiest is if we slowly get up and walk down to my car and we take a ride down the street and you can answer a few questions. Do you have an issue with that?'

'Ah, no, but, questions about what?'

'Why don't we save it for the station? Too many ears around here.'

'Okay, but, what about my truck? And, I'm supposed to be at work.'

'Come with me and don't worry, you can call your boss on the way. And don't worry about your truck. I'm sure it's safe at the store.'

He got up then and tucked his badge back into his jacket. Andrew stood up with him. He moved slowly, unsure of himself. Walking out, Andrew noticed a couple of officers in plain clothes had been hanging around out front. Both of them joined Andrew and the Detective for the journey. One sat next to Andrew in the backseat, but neither spoke to him.

At Quincy police headquarters Andrew was led into a different entrance from that which he'd gone through just days before. The room however was eerily similar to that which he'd given his statement. From the uniforms and small pieces of conversation he heard, it was the Quincy police that walked him in, and one Quincy cop stayed behind in the room. But, it was Detective Harris that did most of the talking, including the chit chat on the car ride in. Andrew felt confused, and was more than a little nervous. It was unclear why he was brought there. A man came into the room and explained to Andrew that he was currently there on his own accord and was not yet under arrest. That little spiel only further clouded his understanding. Finally, he and Detective Harris were alone. Although Andrew was skeptical about just how alone they actually were. He'd seen enough cop shows to know there'd be one or two people monitoring behind the glass at least.

'So, you're an interesting guy I have to say Andrew. From what I gathered, you were born in Dublin. Is that right?' the Detective asked

'Ah, yes, I was. My mother's Irish.'

'You live there long?'

'I don't think I lived there at all really. Like I said, my mother's Irish. My father was American. They lived there for a while, but it was only up to the time I was born.'

'So what's that make you, American or Irish?'

'Both I guess.'

'Where's your mother now?'

'She's moved back.'

'Back to Dublin?'

'Well, back to Ireland. But she's not in Dublin. She's in Donegal. Anyway, why do you want to know this? No offense, but I'm confused.'

'No it's okay. I just wanted to understand more about you than what's already on my file.'

Andrew sat back and paused. He was surprised to hear he had anything to do with the Detective's file. 'Well then, why don't you tell me what you already have on file Detective, then I can fill in the gaps.'

Detective Harris shrugged. 'Okay, we can do that.' He flipped over a manila folder that was sitting on the desk and looked through its contents briefly.

He spoke in a conversational tone, though his head remained down as he continued reading. 'Your father, an alcoholic, was beaten to death in a road rage assault in front of your eyes. How old were you when that happened?'

Andrew tried not to flinch and answered calmly. 'I was around twelve I think. Possibly younger.'

The Detective just shook his head. 'And you had a

brother die from a heroin overdose. You were nineteen?'

'Sounds right.' He answered.

'I'll admit, you definitely had it rough. Andrew shrugged and averted his eyes.

'If you say so.'

'What? Are you saying those things didn't affect you?'

'No. I'm not saying that. It's just that . . . I'm saying what I've been through is not that uncommon around here. Shit, half the people I know have alcoholic fathers and brothers or sisters with drug problems.'

'Is that right? Well at least there's the other half that are doing okay.'

'Nah, the other half are on drugs themselves.'

'Oh yeah? Why do you think that is?'

'Honestly, I think the city . . . no, the entire country turns a blind eye to the drug trade. Why's it so easy to get prescription drugs? There's not enough aunties with cancer to pilfer from, so they're coming from somewhere.'

'Sounds like an indictment on law enforcement. You sure you're in the right place to make a statement like that?'

'I'm sorry sir, but you asked me my opinion Detective.'

'Detective Harris shuffled his feet under the table and leaned forward on his elbows.

'That's right, I did. And let me ask you another question now too.'

He reached down and pulled another folder from his case. 'Was Gina O'Neil on drugs?'

'Gina? How should I know?' Andrew asked.

'You knew her didn't you? You two were close I heard.'

'Well yeah, back in school I guess we were close enough, but I hadn't spoken to her in a long time.'

'Until the other night you mean?'

'What?'

'You hadn't spoken to her until the other night.'

'What?' Andrew said again. 'I didn't speak to her. I haven't seen her. I haven't seen her in years actually.'

'Not what I heard.'

'You heard wrong I'm afraid, Detective.'

'Maybe, maybe not.'

Andrew paused. He didn't know what else to say. He was racking his brain to remember seeing Gina, but just couldn't recall. 'How could the Detective have his facts so wrong' he thought.

He spoke again after a minute. 'The officer earlier said I wasn't under arrest.'

'That's right, as of now you're free.'

'Then I'm free to leave?'

'If you want to, then yes.'

'Then Detective, I'm leaving now.'

'Okay Andrew, that's your decision.' He said. He began

gathering up his papers on the desk. He looked up at Andrew and gave him a stern fatherly look. 'Stay Local Andrew.'

Andrew walked quickly down the hall, tailed the whole way by a uniformed officer. He weaved through the corridors, which had become familiar to him at this stage.

He headed out the front door and walked in the direction of Wollaston Beach. It dawned on him outside that his truck wasn't with him, it stayed parked in front of the store at least a mile away. He started walking quickly up the street, taking long strides despite digging his hands in his pockets.

He made it half a mile when one of the two unmarked police cars pulled up next to him again. It slowed to a stop. Andrew knew who it was even before the door swung open and Detective Harris climbed out flashing his badge again, as if they hadn't spent the last hour together.

'Andrew Dawson' he said as he reached around his waist. Andrew paused, unsure what to say or whether to move. He watched the Detective's hand move back to the front, carrying a set of handcuffs. 'You're under arrest Andrew, for the murder of Gina O'Neil.'

He continued speaking, Andrew could hear him and knew his rights were being read, but he wasn't really listening. His mind had glazed over. He felt weak. He pictured himself floating above the actual scene looking down at his body, watching the motions, his hands on the hood of the Crown Victoria. An officer patting him down for any weapons he might have acquired in the ten minutes since he left the station. The whole time, the Detective's lips were moving, but the words were soundless. Andrew shut his eyes and could feel wetness on his lashes as tears rimmed his eyelids, not falling yet, but gathering heavy around them. And for the first time in recent memory, maybe since childhood, Andrew began to pray.

CHAPTER TEN

Andrew sat staring at a heavy beige door, willing it to open. He waited twenty minutes already in a small rectangular room with no windows. Meanwhile his court appointed attorney signed some paperwork and spoke with the prison officer just outside the room. His patience had long since left him. In a whirlwind forty-eight hours he had been arrested and arraigned on murder charges. It was exhausting. Emotionally, he was breaking down. Physically, he was following shortly behind that. 'Murderer' he thought. 'I've never so much as hurt a fly in my entire life.'

The police apparently had evidence that linked him to the crime. He imagined the investigation carried on at full scale, people in haz-mat suits furiously searching for physical evidence to tie him to the murder, to strengthen a case that at its foundation had to be wrong. 'Doyle's knife' was the only thought that kept running through his head. 'It had to be this guy Doyle.'

He was arraigned and entered a 'not-guilty' plea. A request for bail was denied. The court appointed attorney said it was due to the seriousness of the charge and also that he was seen as a flight risk. 'If I wasn't before, I definitely am now' he thought. He spent the last thirty-six hours locked up in Wyngate Correctional Facility. He was given orange scrubs to wear that signified he was a pre-trial inmate. Jurisdictional rules required that pre-trial inmates be isolated from convicted inmates at all times. Whether or not that was the intention, the jail's excessive population made it a difficult requirement to enforce. When Andrew arrived he was shown to a cell built for one person, but already holding two. He was given a pop-up mattress that the inmates called 'canoes' to sleep in. He laid there the last two nights, but on the whole, sleep evaded him. It helped him a little to think that most County inmates were short-timers, serving for misdemeanor offenses. It was the state facilities that held the more severe prisoners.

He heard voices outside the door grow louder and heard the door buzz and then click open. A Correctional Officer opened the door and held it for the young attorney that the court appointed to handle Andrew's case. He entered the room and pulled out the chair across from Andrew at the small table. 'Hi Andrew.'

'Hi Barry.'

Barry put his brief case on the table top but left it closed. 'Did you sleep any better last night?'

'Not really, no. Would you be able to sleep if you were me?' he asked.

'Okay Andrew, that's too bad. I spoke with one of the warden's representatives about the arrangement.' They assured me that you'll be moved to a double bunk room as soon as one is available.'

'Okay. Thanks then. Is there any update on my case?'

'There's no significant updates, no. The district attorney's office is making sure they're handling it slowly and by the book because of its . . . profile.'

'So they still think I'm guilty then?'

'It's my understanding that they believe you're guilty. They're in the process of handing over all available evidence for the defense to review, but they're also continuing with the investigation to try and cover all angles. They'll likely try and speak with you again.'

'But you'll be here for any future meetings right?'

'Yes. You shouldn't be talking to anyone without me.'

'Okay.' Andrew said. 'So, what are the papers saying? Does everyone think I've done this?'

'I wouldn't worry too much about what the media's saying right now Andrew.'

'But, do they have my name?' he asked.

The lawyer brought his hand up to his face and brushed the hair from his forehead with his thumb before answering. 'They have your name, yes. People are talking. It's best for now that you don't listen.' He answered.

Andrew put his face into his hands and rubbed his eyes hard with his palms. He felt the blood drain from his face and his head was light.

'Are you going to puke?'

Andrew couldn't answer with words, but waved him off as he turned to the side and tried to regain control of his breathing. After a minute, he restored his composure and turned back towards the attorney.

'There's one other thing I wanted to run by you Andrew. I'm getting some questions about your relationship with John Bishop. It's small, but it may be a bargaining chip. Not on sentencing, considering the charge, but we may be able to negotiate small concessions if you can give helpful information on Bishop, you know, like anything you might have about his operations.'

Andrew forced himself to straighten his posture. The implication that he and Bishop were connected bothered him. 'I think there's a misunderstanding Barry. I don't have a relationship with Bishop.'

'The police don't think that's the case.'

'Listen, he was brother's friend when I was a child. I

haven't even seen him in probably two or three years. If I had something on Bishop, believe me, I'd gladly hand it over to them. And I'd do it for free.' He said.

'Okay Andrew. Just keep it mind. Like I said, it could be useful.'

'What about Mike Doyle?' Andrew asked. 'Have the police even bothered following that up?' The attorney slid back in his chair and snipped the top button of his suit jacket closed. 'I communicated to them everything you shared with me Andrew. I've been told they'll look into it, but honestly, and I mean this in the most constructive way possible . . . you're not the first person in here to start naming names after an arrest.'

Andrew shrugged. The more time he spent with the young attorney, the more resentful he grew towards him. He was beginning to find everything he said and did patronizing and was nearly certain the man did not believe that he was innocent. He wasn't sure if that mattered in court, but it mattered to Andrew and it bothered him.

'So are we done for now then?' Andrew asked.

'Yes. I'll be in touch soon with any progress. Remember, don't talk to anyone without me present. Oh, and I'll follow up on that whole bed situation.'

'Yeah thanks Barry.' Andrew said. He heard the door buzz again and click open. The same officer opened it and let the attorney out. Andrew waited again, knowing the guard would be in shortly to take him back to his cell. He felt truly alone and overwhelming dread took hold of him as he pictured Bernadette sitting at her kitchen table, looking at his face in the newspaper under some daunting headline splashed across the page to get a passive reader's attention. He hoped that she knew him well enough to know it couldn't be him. He hoped she, at least, believed it wasn't true.

CHAPTER ELEVEN

Andrew's eyes fully adjusted to the darkness within his cell in the early morning hours. He'd been awake most of the night for the third day in a row. The prison produced its own noises in the dark. Those sounds frightened him deeply and grew no less ominous as they became more familiar. The prison was built in the 1950's. Andrew overheard other inmates' conversations of rumors that it originally housed a mental institution and was extended and repurposed in the 1970's to combat the overcrowding in existing jails. As ghost stories went, Wyngate's was a good one. The sounds throughout the night were attributed to voices and screams echoing from earlier times as opposed to hissing and grating from bad pipework and rusting metal. Stories or not, the place was unnerving to Andrew.

He heard a sound against the cell door and listened to the latch unhinge as he lay in the makeshift cot. It didn't feel quite like the wake up time, but it was difficult to judge with the rectangular door window the only view from within the cell. An officer entered and whispered 'Dawson'.

Andrew sat up quickly to show he was awake. 'I'm here.'

'No shit. Here get up and get anything that might be yours, including your shit tickets. We have a bed for you in another cell.'

Andrew got up quickly. He didn't have much with him since he didn't like venturing to the canteen. He grabbed the small blue recycling bin that was issued to him. In it was his toothbrush, toothpaste, his one roll of toilet paper and a stick of deodorant. He picked it up and followed the prison officer out of the cell. There were two others outside the cell with him. He walked behind the main one and in front of the two others down a long hall to the end, then down a set of stairs. They went through another set of doors into a different wing of the facility. Andrew was unsure of himself. Not that he'd enjoyed the first area they put him, but there was some level of comfort in the separation that the pre-trial wing held from convicted inmates. The officer stopped outside a cell that was close to the entrance of the wing and radioed to a supervisor to confirm the cell's location. He unlocked the latch with a key that looked to belong in medieval times and opened the large steel door. 'Here Dawson' he pointed. 'The bottom bunk has freed up.'

Andrew walked into the cell. It was close to a mirror image of the previous one except there was no canoe set up on the floor. He looked around the small room. He saw the top bunk's occupant was stirring awake. He noticed the color of the scrubs folded over the edge of the bed differed from his own. 'Excuse me sir' Andrew asked the officer 'I thought pre-trial inmates were supposed to be kept separate from convicted inmates?' He pointed over at the different colored uniform.

The officer raised his eyebrows and stiffened his lips before answering. He pointed up at the man in the bunk. 'He's not a convicted inmate. He's an ICE inmate. Consider him in transit.'

'What's an ICE inmate?' Andrew asked.

'Ask him. I'm sure he'll tell you all about it.' The officer answered. He stepped out of the cell and started to close the door. Before he did, he said 'Be glad I didn't throw you in with a skinner. But don't worry you'll meet plenty of them in Walpole once you're convicted.' Lastly he said 'You probably have an hour 'til chow.'

'Okay.' Andrew said.

The door slammed shut loudly and Andrew heard the large key turn the lock back into place. He walked over to the bottom bunk and slid into it. 'An hour until chow' he thought. 'Okay, so it's five am.' In his short time, he was beginning to understand that the prison was built on routine. Everyday every activity followed a strict schedule.

From six to six thirty they got breakfast. Meals where wheeled down in giant carts by inmate workers. They lined up, picked up the food trays from the cart and ate in the cells. From seven to nine am, they were locked down. At nine, there was rec time either in the common room in the housing unit or the adjoining rec yard that held a weight bench, half-court basketball and a handball court. Then lunch was brought in the same manner as breakfast, let out again at one for rec, back in lock down at two, dinner at four, back in lock down until six, then free to roam around in the rec area until lights out at ten. He had been warned to stay cautious during this evening free time. The inmates had four hours to play with. If something was going down, it was likely happening during that period. Andrew didn't feel he needed warnings to remain cautious. His shoulders felt permanently tensed and his eyes darted around rapidly since he'd arrived. He didn't go out of his way to make conversation and for the most part no one spoke to him. He guessed much of that had to do with word getting around about what he was being charged with.

Others did make some small talk, seemingly just to pass the time. He was in no hurry for time to pass. In fact, he wished it froze days ago while he sat on his porch with Bernadette. His new cell mate didn't say much that morning. He basically avoided eye contact altogether. By the time they were locked down after lunch however, he had started to chip in a few words. Andrew figured boredom had probably gotten the best of him. He assumed most people broke down and talked to their cell mates eventually, regardless of what each was being held for. It wasn't natural to be in a confined place with another human being. Something had to break that awkwardness.

'You're pre-trial right?' the man asked.

'Yeah, I am.' Andrew answered.

'I guess that's obvious with the orange suit.'

Andrew nodded 'What's the blue mean? The CO said you were ice or something. I didn't know what he was talking about.'

'You never heard of ICE?'

'No, should I have?'

'I don't know. You would if you were illegal here. It stands for Immigration and Customs Enforcement.'

'So you're illegal.'

'Well, yeah. I've lived here over ten years, but I don't have a green card. They picked me up in Dallas trying to get on a plane back to Logan. I was on holidays in Texas.'

'Shit. What'd they pick you up for?'

'Just for being in the country, no other crime or anything.'

'And what, they sent you back to Massachusetts to sort

it out.'

The man laughed, but Andrew felt it wasn't one of amusement. 'I wish. I sat in a Texas prison cell for a month while they kicked my case around the county, state and federal courts.'

'Sounds a little extreme.'

'More than a little. It's safe to say ICE is a federal power that's at best, unchecked. Fucksake, they spend millions each year just to move us back and forth. This place is getting some of those dollars for every day that I'm held here. It's like they're renting jail space until they can figure out whether to leave me be or ship me back to Mayo.'

Andrew nodded in understanding. 'Yeah, well, sorry to hear that.'

The man climbed back up to the top bunk and laid back down 'Thanks.'

Andrew took this to mean the conversation was over. He guessed that lock down time was winding down and stood up to peak out the door slat. When he turned back around, he noticed the man cautiously watching him. He averted his eyes when Andrew turned back, but he'd seen the look the man gave him. He also felt it. He sensed fear from that look and realized his cell mate must've heard from other inmates or the officers about what charge Andrew was being held on. He felt shame just thinking about the accusation. Although, he was somewhat glad that no one had asked him about it. He knew in his heart that he was innocent. Whenever he felt the urge to try and convince others of this, he thought of how shallow a stranger's words would come across to them. 'How many more before me screamed their innocence from the rooftops? How many of them were actually guilt free?' So he held back. He said nothing, because talking about it to inmates and convicts wasn't going to help. He needed help, and he needed it fast. As to how he could find it, it was too bad his mind continually drew a blank.

At six pm the cell doors were unlocked for the last time that day and the inmates poured out from their units into the block's common areas. Andrew remained in his cell with the door open. He stayed lying on the bed just staring at the metal springs on the bottom of the bunk above him. For twenty minutes he laid there, listening to the voices outside the cell. Some were deep murmurs, others were pitchy, but none were very clear. He made out a few conversations in that time. One he heard was an inmate complaining to another about being forced to wear bobos. Bobos, he gleaned, were the standard issue jail shoes that were more like Velcro slippers with plastic bottoms. The inmate was pissed off because his mother hadn't put cash on his canteen account. That meant he couldn't pick up a pair of the white Reebok classics, which they sold in the commissary. The bobos made his feet sweat apparently. He heard another man with a nasally voice calling one of the inmates a banker, which Andrew picked out of context had something to do with feeding information to the prison officers.

After a while, straining to listen to conversations grew tiresome. He sat up on the bed, careful not to hit his head on the bunk above and planted his feet on the ground. He stood up and walked slowly over to the cell's doorway and looked out. He took in the scene around him. There were small groups scattered around the common area in conversations. Others lounged in communal chairs alone, either flicking through books or just staring into space. He watched several men walk in from the outdoor area and join some of the already formed groups. There were a mix of uniform colors, but most were brown. Andrew wasn't sure what those or the other's signified. Part of him wanted to know, part could live without finding out. There were a few others in orange, but not many and those there appeared to be alone like him.

Andrew walked out of the cell slowly and made his way down a small set of stairs. Through quick glances, he saw some people take notice of him as he passed, but none acknowledged him outwardly. He assumed it was a defense mechanism that was learned in these places quickly. Look, but be fast and avoid eye contact. He felt that in three days, he needed eyes in the back of his head to survive in there. He walked outside and took a seat in a small set of benches in between the weights area and the handball court. A few inmates worked out, while a couple others looked to be playing HORSE on the basketball court. Others just stood around, Andrew imagined, taking the time to breathe in fresh air while the opportunity existed.

Andrew was looking at his own pair of bobos down on his feet when a shadow passed over him and he felt the bench shift slightly as a man sat close to him. 'Too close' Andrew thought. He looked young and old at the same time. He was really thin Andrew noticed, and had a close cropped bowl cut that made him look like a teenager. His face was gaunt however, and it cast a vampiric hue. That face made him appear older than his thin frame suggested.

'Hey new blood' the man asked. 'You carrying? Hook me up?'

Andrew didn't know what to say so just shook his head no and shrugged.

'Come on dude, I know got that stop sign. Hook a brother up, I'm fucking fiending here.'

'Sorry man, I don't what you're talking about.' Andrew said and tried to shift away slowly to his left.

107

'Aw fuck you then dude.'

Andrew heard another, deeper voice from behind him. 'Get lost Pete!'

The skinny guy looked over toward the voice, then got up and walked back inside. The other man came around and took his spot on the bench. 'Don't mind Pete, he's just one of the junkies. They're like part of the furniture in here and always looking for handouts.'

Andrew nodded. He was glad Pete took off, but not exactly comfortable with his new visitor either. The man was much larger than Pete, close to Andrew's size, but broader and Andrew thought 'Denser?' He had a healthy complexion compared to Pete too. He wore a neatly trimmed beard and had a set of forearms that went straight into his palms, which Andrew noticed. The lack of wrists suggested great strength and looked dangerous.

Andrew swallowed saliva that had built up in his throat and gathered enough courage to speak. He asked, 'What's 'stop sign'? That guy said I had to have stop sign on me.'

'Stop sign is suboxone.' The man answered.

Andrew was confused. 'The rehab drug?'

'Exactly, except it ain't for rehab in here. It's used for getting high.'

Andrew asked 'Is it allowed in here?'

'Fuck no kid, but it's here. The skids will smuggle it

anyway they can. They crush it into paste and have their kids use it for art projects and send daddy pictures made from the shit to hang on his cell wall. CO's are even stripping stamps off the mail cause it can be used to seal them on the envelopes.'

'Wow . . . shit.' Andrew said. He was amazed, but not surprised by the ingenuity and brazen tactics that drug addicts employed. He had seen some of it firsthand.

He noticed suddenly that the sun had been swept aside for much dimmer moonlight, though the air remained warm in the dark. He looked around the yard and saw that most of those inmates that were outside had headed indoors except for two stragglers plus the man next to him on the bench. It dawned on him that the two men kept looking over in his direction. Every few seconds they looked over, then away, then at the doorway, and then back again.

He felt the hair on the back of his neck stand up and a tingling feeling ran down his arms. 'Something's wrong' he thought. As he thought it, he saw a brief flash of light in his periphery when the moonlight caught metal that shimmered in the man's hand next to him.

Andrew jumped to his feet just in time to dodge a swipe that came across the man's body. The man was off balance from the miss and Andrew took the advantage and kicked the bench as hard as he could, knocking it backwards and sending the man falling over with it. He turned to find the two stragglers almost upon him. He had no time to move, so he tightened his body and absorbed the blows as both men hit him at the same time tackling him to the ground. The three of them hit the pavement with momentum and rolled. Andrew kicked out at both of them from the ground, while covering his head with his arms. His kicks were wild, but accurate enough to land, catching one man in the face and the other in his testicles. Both fell away, but not before landing several punches to Andrew's face. The adrenaline blocked any immediate pain from the blows, but he tasted blood that ran down from his nose, over his lips and into his mouth. He scrambled to get up, landing a heavy kick to the man's head that had fallen closest to him as he rose. He spun around frantically searching for his original attacker. Andrew knew that he was the main worry.

He turned just in time to see the man lunge at him with the blade again. This time Andrew dove out of the way and rolled over next to the weight bench. He reached around on the ground, searching for anything he could use to defend himself. The man ran at him again. Andrew reached for a short metal dumbbell, a detached pole the length of his forearm with no weights connected. He stood up and braced himself, feeling the weight of steel in his hand. The man plunged forward with the knife. Andrew side stepped it this time, brushing it aside with his left hand, then came down hard with the steel pole onto the man's forearm. He heard a crack and saw the knife fall from his hand. It was small and looked homemade, more a shiv than a knife. Andrew paused only for a second. He heard commotion behind him as the officers on duty rushed out and grabbed hold of the other assailants. In that second he saw into his attackers eyes. First he saw pain, from what Andrew assumed was a broken wrist. He hoped to see fear next. He was wrong. Anger overtook the pain in the man's eyes in that second. Andrew only knew one way to stop it and he swung the steel pole hard again. Officers tackled him to the ground at the same time, but not before he heard the crunch of a jaw breaking and watched shards of broken teeth fall before him like snowflakes as his face was shoved hard into the ground.

CHAPTER TWELVE

A staff doctor worked each day during normal daytime hours. In evenings and overnight however, there generally wasn't a need at Wyngate. There were tough guys in there, but most were serving short time. That alone seemed to stem some of the violence that ran rampant in other longer term state and federal facilities. Plus, with Boston about thirty minutes away, not to mention several other hospitals within ten to fifteen miles, the prison budget couldn't afford doctors working twenty four hour shifts. There was a medic on every shift however. Also, it was required that at all times a certain number of correctional officers with medical certifications were scheduled.

The infirmary was more like an office. It reminded Andrew of a nurse's office at his old high school except the medic was male and the supplies were a grade above Tylenol and Midol. Since the attack in the prison yard, his heart beat like a bass drum. It was loud enough to effect his hearing.

No number of breathing exercises or reassurances from the medic seemed to calm him down. Initially, he worried that the men that came after him would strike again, especially if they also ended up in the infirmary. He asked multiple officers about this and each had the same answer. One of the men was in isolation, while the other two were taken to Massachusetts General Hospital. One man had a concussion. The other man was hurt more seriously, with a broken wrist and broken jaw, not to mention several broken teeth. Andrew also kept pressing the officers to explain why the men attacked him. The only answer he got was that those guys were short-timers. They were local men, with daughters of their own. Andrew knew men like them. He knew that they weren't trying to send a message. Their only aim was to take him down. He could see it from their side. He could nearly empathize with them. At the same time, he knew they had the wrong man, although there'd never be the opportunity to explain that to them.

Andrew wanted to believe that under normal circumstances he'd feel bad for what he'd done. He thought he'd experience at least trace levels of guilt. However, current circumstances were well beyond normal. He felt his actions were justified and necessary. Mostly, he was just glad that he wasn't also lying in a hospital bed. 'It very nearly could've been the morgue.' He thought. His injuries weren't serious. His nose had been bloodied and it swelled badly along with both eyes, but luckily, nothing was broken. He imagined he looked much worse than he felt. His head was in some pain, but that was probably more related to coming down after a stressful situation.

After he was cleaned up, he was walked down to a different area of the prison. It wasn't openly stated to him, but he guessed the prison now considered him a target. 'Should have known that already.' He thought. He assumed he was now in protective custody as they miraculously found him a cell for himself in a separate wing and officers seemed to be around him much more frequently than the previous three days.

Whether it was the body's release after the fight or just being alone finally in a cell on his own, he slept much better that night. He made it straight through the night without waking once. Also, he had no dreams, good or bad, that he remembered. That morning he felt refreshed. There were aches and pains of course, but he felt well rested at least and believed his mind was sharper than it had been for days. It was like a fog that cloaked his thinking had finally dissipated with the rising sun.

Breakfast was brought to him and he ate in his cell. He was locked down longer in the morning than usual. When he was let out, he was allowed to walk around the common area, but he was flanked by two officers the entire time. Andrew noticed a slight change with the officers who were around him. Something about their demeanor towards him was different than it had been before. He was unsure why. 'Surely, it had nothing to do with the fight.' He thought. He considered whether it was all in his head. He asked himself whether it was just his perception of how they acted towards him, had that changed since now his mind was functioning more clearly.

As the morning passed and the day wore on however, he put aside the notion that it was all in his head. While they weren't exactly nice to him, they were no longer as cold towards him. Some were more talkative it seemed and others appeared more relaxed around him now. There was no mistaken that there was a difference overnight.

After lunch an officer came and got him from the cell and said he had a visitor. He was led down a series of corridors until he came to a locked-down room in between the attorney meeting rooms and the contact visit area. He was informed by one of the officers that he was allowed visitors, but that pre-trial inmates could only talk to visitors behind glass. Next, he was led to a seat in one of the booths at the end and told he needed to speak and listen through the phone.

He sat down and picked up the receiver. He cradled it

on his shoulder while he waited. Through the phone's ear, he heard a buzzing noise as a visitor was let into the room and led to the booth on the chair opposite him, protected by glass.

Bernadette picked up the phone and looked at Andrew. He could see her eyes search his face and take in his injuries. He watched helplessly as she started to cry. Tears filled his eyes as well. Seeing her at all was a shock to him. Seeing her crying across from him, behind a protective glass barrier was nearly too painful to bear. He spoke into the receiver.

'Bernie.' He said

She looked up at him and tried to choke back the sobs. Finally she managed to hold them back and she wiped the tears from both sides of her face with her free hand. 'I'm sorry.' She said.

Andrew wasn't really sure how to continue. He wasn't certain what she knew or whether she thought he did what the papers said he did. He stayed silent. She continued finally. 'I had to come . . . I had to see you. Just . . . your face. You're hurt.'

Slowly he answered. 'I'm glad you came . . . this' he said and pointed to his face, 'don't worry about this. Honestly it looks much worse than it feels.

'I sure hope so. I mean, it looks really bad.' She gave him a small smile through her flushed cheeks.

Andrew laughed lightly and smiled back. He felt pain from the bruises on his face when he did. 'So, that's why you came here? To insult my looks?'

'No. But that doesn't mean I'd pass up the opportunity.'

'Of course.' He said. 'So . . . how are you?'

'Andrew'

'What?'

'That's not why I'm here either. I don't want to small talk.'

'Okay. Well then, what is it?'

'You know my uncle, the attorney.'

'Um. Yeah, I don't know him, but I remember meeting him before.'

'You did, I'm sure of it. Anyway, he's a defense attorney. Like, a really good one. He's taken over your case.'

'What? How . . . why?'

'I . . . um, I spent the last few days crying at his feet to get him to do it. That's how.'

'Really?' He felt awkward, but grateful nonetheless. 'Thank you. But, I guess . . . why would you do that?'

'Andrew' she said sternly 'You're my friend for one, and you're innocent. I asked about your court appointed attorney. He's not bad, just not as experienced.'

'Wait, you know I'm innocent. You didn't believe what was in the news?' he asked.

'Of course I know you're innocent Andrew, I know you, plus . . .'

'Plus what?'

'I saw you Andrew. I'm your eye witness, or, your alibi.'

Andrew looked around him to see if the officer was listening. He wasn't sure if the conversation was being recorded, but he said it anyway. 'Bernie, I am innocent. But, Gina was killed Thursday. I saw you on Friday night, not Thursday.'

'You don't understand.'

'What don't I understand? Please, explain it to me. I don't want to see you taking a fall for me.'

'You didn't see me Thursday, but I saw you.'

Andrew sat up straighter, pushing his eyebrows close together in confusion.

Bernadette continued talking, 'I came to see you Thursday night too. I knocked on your door. I could see you. You must've fallen asleep watching television on the couch. I waited. I waited for over an hour on your porch, deciding what to do. When the snow started falling heavily, I decided to leave.' She paused. 'I'm sorry, it's embarrassing.'

'Bernie' he said and leaned forward towards the glass 'it's not embarrassing. You just saved my life. So the cops, you've gone to them with this?'

'My uncle and I did yes. Well to them and the District

Attorney. The timeline fits Andrew. They're letting you go.'

Andrew was stunned. He felt weak and light headed from excitement. Had he been standing, he thought, he would've fallen over. He ran his palm over his eyes to hold back tears that welled up, and then ran his hand through his hair. 'I can't believe it.' He said 'when?'

'I think there's some paperwork and stuff they've been working on all morning, but it should be soon, at least within twenty four hours.'

'I don't know what to say. Thank you Bernie, I can't believe it.'

'There's one other thing though Andrew. It's not good, but there's another factor to why you're getting out.'

'What is it?' he said concerned suddenly that he'd been dreaming and this was all part of a sick joke.

'There's been another one.' She said.

'Another what?' he asked

She paused for moment before speaking into the phone 'Another girl found. Lisa Stark.'

Andrew looked up at Bernadette, but didn't say anything for a moment. Memories flashed into his head of another precocious, smiling young girl he had known in his youth. 'Lisa Stark' he said. 'She was in school with us too.'

CHAPTER THIRTEEN

Andrew walked out of Wyngate Correctional Facility the following Monday morning. The day that greeted him was wet, but warm. He walked out in his work boots, jeans and hooded sweatshirt, the same way he walked in. The rest of his belongings were handed to him in a big brown envelope, which he emptied out and tossed outside of the gate. Stevie greeted him outside. Andrew was glad to see a friend's face the moment he was freed. Stevie drove in with Andrew's truck, which he picked up from impound a day earlier after it had been combed through for evidence. He offered the keys to Andrew, but he wasn't interested in getting behind the wheel. Andrew got comfortable in the passenger's seat and watched the trees blur by out the window on the highway as they drove back to Quincy. Stevie tried to make small talk, but didn't force it. Andrew noticed and appreciated that he kept the topics light, like recapping the Bruins games he missed during the week.

They pulled up outside of Andrew's apartment. Stevie

handed the keys over to him and Andrew asked, 'You need the truck to get home?' 'Actually' Stevie answered 'I thought I'd stay with you a few days and help you get settled. If you're cool with it.'

Andrew stood for a moment swinging the keys around his finger in short intervals considering the request. 'Yeah Stevie.' He said 'it'd be good to have a friend around, thanks.' Andrew walked into the apartment to find it clean. The spare room had already been cleared out for Stevie and he found fresh milk in the refrigerator and a loaf of bread on the counter. Stevie watched him look around for a moment, then took a seat on the couch. 'I had your spare key. So when Bernie told me you'd be getting out, I wanted to make sure the place was clean and everything, ya know.'

'Thanks Stevie, I appreciate it. You ah . . . you talk to Bernie since?' Stevie shook his head. 'Afraid not brother. She called me to let me know when you were getting out. That's all. I think she got a bit of shit from her fiancé for . . . you know, getting involved and everything.'

'I take it they're still together though right?' Andrew asked. A glimmer of hope crept into his chest followed sharply by guilt. Stevie looked at him with an apologetic smile and nudged his shoulders. 'I know man.' Andrew said, 'don't know what I was thinking.' He stood in the doorway between the kitchen and living room and reached his arms up to stretch them against the frame. 'You heard about Lisa Stark I take it.' He asked. 'I did.' Stevie answered. 'You wanna . . . talk about that stuff now?'

'No actually, I don't. Just that, this dude's out there still you know?' He paused for a few seconds, then continued, 'Hey you uh, you been around this Doyle guy since?' He asked. 'It was his fucking knife that jammed me up, I know it. Well, I don't know it-know it, like for a fact I mean, but . . . I can feel it.'

Stevie shook his head slowly. 'I haven't seen or heard from him since that day you saw us outside Bishop's place. To be honest, he and I squared up on the work I did for him then and there. It's not like we were buddies or anything, you know.'

Andrew nodded his head and took his arms down from the wall. 'Yeah man. I know. Listen, I can't even think about it right now. I'm gonna take a shower and stuff. You good here for a few on your own?'

'I've made myself at home Andrew as you can see. Do what you need to do, I'll hang here.'

Having Stevie in the apartment with him helped Andrew to start to feel himself again. They danced around the topic of Lisa Stark, Gina O'Neil and the others several times over the next couple days, especially when something would show up in the news in the evenings. Andrew couldn't really stomach the topic for longer than a minute. He stopped watching any channel on television that even remotely showed news and he tossed his cell phone off the back porch into the trees behind the house after making the mistake of checking his Facebook page and looking at the newspaper online. His release made the news, but with much less fanfare than his capture. He was page five material at best when he walked out of Wyngate.

He was still waiting to hear if his old boss would take him back to work, which felt less likely with every passing day. He insisted that Stevie should go to work that week instead of moping around the apartment with him. There was still a stigma around him, especially with another girl found dead and no one else in custody for that or the other murders. He felt the eyes him when he walked into the shop or went to the gas station. Basically anytime he stepped out of the house he got looks. Innocent until proven guilty might work in the courts, but not in the media and not in the public's eyes.

He was emotionally worn down by Saturday. Stevie wasn't working on the weekend, so he talked Andrew into going out for some food around lunch time. It was the first time in over a day that Andrew agreed to go outside. They drove down to a local deli that they frequented since teenagers and grabbed a small table in the corner of the dining room. Andrew grabbed the seat with his back to the wall. There weren't many people in for a Saturday, but he still felt eyes on him when he entered. He thought to himself 'it'd be better if it was jammed with people, no one would probably notice me then.' He could see the lingering stares in his periphery. He wasn't sure if it was real or his imagination, but he could sense hostility in the air. He stayed seated as Stevie walked up to the counter, ordered their lunch and paid. The line was short, so Stevie was back over in less than five minutes. In that time, Andrew sat hunched over, trying his best to look small and unnoticeable. He kept bringing his hands up over his face, rubbing his chin or scratching his forehead. Stevie sat down in his chair and looked over at him. 'What's up man? You look like a cornered squirrel. You okay?'

'I don't know Stevie. I'm tired of people shooting daggers through me with their eyes. Can't take this shit much longer.'

'Hang in there man. You didn't do anything wrong. It'll just take time, that's all.' Stevie said. Andrew took in a deep breath and let it out slowly. He leaned forward across the table and said in a quiet voice, 'You think time is gonna make people forget that I was arrested and charged with fucking murder Stevie? Really?' Stevie just shrugged.

Andrew sat back a little in his chair. 'Sorry Stevie. I'm not trying take anything out on you.' 'Hey man' Stevie said. 'Don't worry about me, you're going through some shit, I get that.'

'Where's the food anyway?' Andrew asked. Stevie started playing with the napkin holder. Andrew thought he wanted to say more, but didn't press him. 'What? Oh, yeah, they'll bring it over.' Stevie answered. A second later they both turned to look up at a man standing over their table, casting a shadow over the middle of it. Neither had seen him approaching, but both noticed him now. He was tall and wore a dark button down shirt with the top few buttons undone so that chest hair and a thin gold chain peeked out over the cloth. Andrew and Stevie both sat looking up at him, but he didn't say anything right away. He reached into his pocket and pulled out a receipt, which he slapped onto the table. Then he pulled out a roll of bills and counted out the amount from the receipt and laid it on top.

'What the fuck is that?' Stevie asked and pointed to the cash on the table. 'That's your money back.' The man answered. 'I know it's my money back, I'm more curious of the why?'

'I'm the manager here and I'm refusing to serve you two that's why.'

'What? Are you fucking kidding me? We've been coming

here for years.' Stevie said.

'I know perfectly well who you are. He's not welcome in here.' He said and pointed to Andrew. 'Now, I'm asking you nicely to leave.'

'This is asking us fucking nicely?' Stevie said. The man put his hands on the table and leaned closer towards them. 'I don't want a scene here. So just take off. Go somewhere else please.' Stevie swiped his own hand quickly across the surface and picked up a fork and jammed it into the table. The man pulled his hand back off the table just in time. Stevie jumped up from his seat and lunged forward with an elbow towards the man's chest. Andrew jumped up too and grabbed Stevie across the table holding him back, but just barely. 'Leave it Stevie.' Andrew said. 'Let's just go.' Stevie was breathing heavy. His eyes were locked on the tall man, who was trying to stand his ground, but looked weak all of sudden and Andrew saw fear in his eyes. 'Stevie!' Andrew said more firmly. Stevie shook his head finally and broke his stare from the man. He looked over to Andrew. After a few seconds he nodded. 'Yeah Andrew. Fuck this place.' He grabbed the cash off the table and stuffed it into his pocket. Stevie shoved the chair hard under the table. The loud 'bang' drew the remaining looks from the few that hadn't already turned their attention to the altercation. Stevie brushed past the manager as he walked out and gave him one last fervent stare. Andrew followed closely behind Stevie. He was braced to interfere with any sudden rush Stevie might attempt just in case. They walked out the door slowly, but without further incident and went around back to get the truck.

Stevie lightened when they were back in traffic. 'You wanna try someplace else?' Andrew looked over at him and shook his head. 'Nah man. I think I'll just head back. Order a pizza or something, I don't care.'

They lounged back at Andrew's apartment watching television and not really saying much for the rest of the day. Andrew kept running over the last week in his head. He couldn't focus on anything else. 'Time might change things, sure' he thought. 'but how much time.' The more he considered it, the more appealing it became to him. He needed to disappear. He couldn't take the looks, the sneers, the judgment any longer, at least not now. 'I need to just go' he thought. 'Just start fresh somewhere else, somewhere that no one knows my face.'

He got up and walked to the refrigerator and grabbed two bottles of beer and opened them. He threw the caps in the trash and walked into the living room. He sat on the couch adjacent to Stevie and reached over and handed him one of the beers. Stevie took it from his hand and gave him a questioning look as he sat down. 'I need to go Stevie.'

Stevie gave Andrew a puzzled look. 'Now? Where?' Andrew shook his head. 'No, you're not getting me. I mean, I need to go somewhere else. Get away for a while, you know what I mean? Like, start fresh somewhere.'

Stevie leaned forwards and put the beer down on the coffee table in front of him. 'Come on Andrew. I told you, time is all. It'll take time, but this shit will blow over.'

'I don't think so Stevie. And, I can't just hide in my apartment here until it does man. I'm a fucking prisoner still, afraid to walk out of this place.'

'Who gives a shit what these people think man? Really, they don't know you.' Stevie said.

'Stevie, I give a shit! Everyone in this fucking city, shit, probably even the state has seen my face and associates me with one thing. I can't live in fucking shame any longer!'

'So . . . your gonna leave. Just leave everything you know?'

'Yeah. I think I am.'

'Where you gonna go then?'

'I don't know really. But . . . when my mother took off, she made me get my Irish passport renewed. I think I might go there. Fuck it. I think I will.'

'And do what man? You need money and shit to even do something like that.'

'Stevie, I've got money. I've been fucking busting my ass working since I was eighteen. I've got enough in the bank.'

'You're all set then huh? I mean what the fuck. What about me?'

Andrew took a long sip from his beer and put it down on the coffee table. 'Stevie, man. You're my best friend. You know that. But really, this ain't about you.' Stevie got up and walked into the spare room. Andrew could hear rustling from the room. A minute later Stevie walked back out with his backpack on his back. 'Dude, come on Stevie. Don't be like that.'

'I'm not being like anything man. You made your mind up Andrew, I can see that.' He walked over towards the doorway. He turned back towards Andrew. 'Just tell me though. You won't stick around for me. What about Bernie? You'd stick around for her I'm sure.'

Andrew leaned forward, then stood up and turned to face Stevie. He knew the answer was yes. Stevie knew it too. But, it's not something he could ever admit to Stevie, as close as they were. Andrew knew his leaving would hit Stevie hard. The guy had no one else, but Andrew. He never knew a father and his mother had disappeared off the face of the earth years ago. Where she'd gone or who with was something Stevie never discussed. Andrew remembered bringing it up to try and comfort him, but a dark cloud seemed to descend over Stevie when he did so Andrew dropped it. 'Too painful.' Andrew thought at the time. He knew the feeling. He had his own pain to contend with. Andrew guessed it was that silently shared pain that drew them to each other and kept them such good friends over the years. He looked over at Stevie. He thought he saw the beginning of tears forming around his eyes. 'I'm sorry Stevie.' He said. Stevie kept his face hard and swallowed. 'Yeah, me too.' he said and turned and walked out the door.

CHAPTER FOURTEEN

Andrew carried a large box from the back of his truck to the storage locker. It was the last of several large boxes he'd packed and loaded into the space. Mostly he packed away clothes and tools. He'd signed his old Ford over to Chef Benson who said he could find use for it and planned to leave it behind the shop on West Elm before heading off. He offered it to Stevie first, but he said he didn't want it. They barely spoke at all since Andrew made his decision to leave. He had some furniture packed away in the storage locker along with the clothes and tools, but not much. Half of what furnished his apartment was borrowed. Most of the rest wasn't worth storing. When he thought about it, he was surprised to find his stuff still in his apartment at all when he was released. He had half assumed that the landlord would have gotten rid of everything to avoid having him on his property. 'Perhaps they were afraid of what they might find there.' He considered.

He thought more about his decision after Stevie had left

his apartment upset and in the days following as he began to get everything together. The factors for his decision hadn't changed one bit and that further solidified his resolve. Stevie would miss him, he knew that, but Bernie was still getting married to another man and his boss had to let him go in order to avoid losing most of his customers.

He didn't want to be recognized every time he stepped from his stoop. 'Not for the current reasons anyway' he thought. 'It would kill me to live like that.'

He reached up and grabbed the metal grate and pulled the shutters down on the locker. He took a knee to close the lock at the notch on the floor. As he was crouched down, he heard a car pull up behind him and turned his body to see it. It was a navy blue sedan and without looking further, he knew who it was. He finished locking the shutters and stood up. He turned around and brushed his hands off on his jeans.

Detective Harris was walking towards him. When Andrew turned to him, the Detective put his hands up and said 'I come in peace.'

Andrew just nodded, but waited for the man to get closer before talking. When he approached Andrew said 'Detective. Can I do something for you?'

'No Andrew, you can't. I just came by to see you off. I heard you were leaving town.'

'Wouldn't you if you were me?' Andrew asked.

The Detective nodded in agreement. 'Yes, I suppose I would if I were you. So, where you headed?'

'Does it matter?' Andrew asked, making it obvious to the Detective that he wasn't up for talking.

'No . . . no, I guess not. Well, I'll let you off then. I genuinely only came by to say hello and goodbye before you took off. Good luck Andrew.' He said.

Andrew sighed. 'One question Detective. Why did you let me walk out that day only to pick me up minutes later?' It was a question that weighed on Andrew heavily. He had initially asked his lawyer about it, but never got clarity as to why. Once he was in prison, other things had taken over his mind. It was only after he knew he was being released that the question began to eat away at him again.

The Detective paused and considered the question for a few seconds before answering. 'I cut you loose because I thought we had the wrong guy Andrew. Soon after I did, the evidence said otherwise . . . looks like I was right after all.'

The Detective started walking away. Andrew wanted to ask more. He wanted to know whether they were any closer to finding the real killer. He wanted to know had they found Doyle. He wondered if they took him serious or just assumed he was giving out any name he could to get the scent off himself. 'No' Andrew thought. He wasn't sure why, but he had a strong feeling that Detective Harris was not one to leave any tip or bit of information un-pursued. He wanted to talk more, to find out and to help. But, his urge to run, to get out while he still could was stronger. 'I'm free.' He said internally, 'Stay that way.' Andrew watched the Detective take a few more steps towards his car, then called after him, 'Dublin.'

'What's that?' Detective Harris asked and turned back towards Andrew.

'I'm going to Dublin. Figured I'd put my Irish passport to use. It's been gathering dust for a while.'

He nodded. 'Good. Dublin's a good city . . . good. Take care Andrew.' He said, then waved and continued towards his car. Andrew waved goodbye, then walked to his truck. 'Nope' he thought. 'I won't miss this place. Not one bit.'

CHAPTER FIFTEEN

There were a handful of memories locked away in the vault of Andrew's mind. Many were painful and those stayed deep within that vault at all costs. Some were embarrassing, which made him blush whenever they rose to the surface. The rest however were just dormant for the reason that they didn't seem important at the time. The Dawson's had visited back and forth to Ireland a few times when Andrew was young, but not since before his father was killed. Everything got harder after that. Vacations grew fewer and further apart. He didn't remember Dublin really, nor should he since most of their trips started with landing at Dublin airport, then driving three hours straight to Donegal. Cities were natural to him after growing up in the Boston area, but Dublin city was still unchartered territory. He wasn't sure what to expect except through bits of information he'd heard from others, mostly his mother, over the years. Although she painted the picture of the 'Big Smoke', a dirty Dublin that probably existed more in her imagination at that time than anywhere else.

Though unfamiliar with Dublin city center, he remembered the airport except that the old terminal building was now overshadowed by a modern state of the art second terminal. The air outside the airport made him nostalgic when he breathed it in. It tasted of damp grass and smoked peat that reminded him of winter visits to Donegal. The early morning was still dark and a mist hung in the air like a cloud in slow descent. Also, it was crisp, jacket weather, as expected in early spring.

He lined up for a taxi and was seated in one on the way into the city within minutes. The journey through Dublin city ran at odds with the serenity offered outside of the airport. In the north inner city many revelers were still out and active, spilling out of nightclubs or fast food restaurants called chip shops. He looked on in amusement counting the rhythm of the street's design, chip shop, pub, chip shop, pub, chip shop, pub. It was an odd city planning strategy, but was not without a certain charm.

O'Connell Street was heavily littered with discarded food wrappers and empty beer cans, mostly Budweiser and Dutch Gold. The trash lessened the impressiveness of the statues that lined the center of the street, while the tall metal poll that the taxi driver called the spire just looked out of place with its historic surroundings. Several statues also had a number of twenty-something men and scantily clad young women loitering around the base. Many looked worn out from a booze-filled night out, while others were locked in loud disagreements. When the driver hit the central lock button, the sharp slam of the knobs had a disconcerting effect that Andrew thought was the opposite of his intention.

They crossed the River Liffey in the cab and Andrew thought to the naked eye it looked to be more of the same, despite what he'd heard of the city's north-south divide. The driver talked the entire journey, explaining much of the route in real time as they drove it. They drove past Trinity College and turned left past a late night burger place and signs for a men's hair clinic shortly after that. The driver explained they needed to take Georges Street, Aungier Street and then Camden Street. Andrew was surprised to learn it was three street names for one road that seemed to be named at arbitrary sections. The road itself was not very long, but the sea of taxi cabs made it nearly impenetrable.

At the corner, the taxi swung around left to Harcourt Street, where Andrew's early morning tour of Dublin ended. Harcourt Street looked to be a business district with Georgian buildings lining both sides of the street. The buildings housed everything from offices, bars, restaurants, hotels, night clubs, coffee shops, art galleries and a police headquarters. Andrew crossed the street to the small hotel that the taxi driver had pointed out to him. He stumbled over a set of tram tracks that he hadn't noticed until he crossed them. He had chosen that hotel online, mainly because of its central location and its affordability. He needed somewhere he could live for up to a week or two until he could find a place to settle. He noticed as he approached, his hotel doubled as a bar and also housed a nightclub on its below street level landing. A couple of doormen still lingered around the entrance, but appeared to only be shepherding out the last remaining stragglers from the club. He slipped past two staggering young men in cheap suits with no ties and started up the steps to the reception area's entrance. As he reached for the door, it flung open quickly and without regard for his face. He blocked it with his arm just in time and noticed a blur charge past him. The door-swinging blur was a woman and she stopped at the bottom of the steps and turned back to him. He must've yelled 'shit' or 'woah' or something like that without realizing. The girl looked at him and asked 'Excuse me?' Andrew thought it came out a little too aggressively.

He gathered himself and turned towards her. She had dark hair that looked nearly black in the night, yet glimmered with a hint of red or auburn from the shine off the orange streetlights. Her skin was very white, not pale or unhealthy white, more porcelain, except for her cheeks, which held a healthy rose blush. Her eyes were red like she had recently been rubbing them and her nose ran slightly like she had been crying. Andrew assumed she had been. He realized he was staring only when she spoke to him again. 'Well?' she said.

'Nothing' he said back and shifted his feet uncomfortably and averted his gaze from her red eyes. 'Just . . . you alright?'

'I'm grand. You're the one staring.' She answered.

Andrew shrugged, 'Sorry' he said 'I'm a little dazed, I just flew in.' Andrew looked down at his bags and kicked one lightly with his foot to draw her attention to them. His discomfort made him feel he needed to point out the obvious.

She followed his eyes down to the bags that sat at his feet. 'Right' she said.

Andrew reached down for his luggage and said. 'Well . . . goodnight.'

She turned then and sat on the stoop. Her fingers held a cigarette she pulled from nowhere and she put it to her lips. She pulled it out again and said up the steps, 'it's morning actually.'

Andrew paused again with the door now held open with his hip. 'Yeah, I guess it is.' He walked into reception, puzzled by the girl's demeanor, but strangely intrigued with her as well. He gave the man at reception his name and credit card. The man swiped his card and handed him back a room key and pointed out the way to the room. 'Will you be looking for breakfast?'

Andrew considered the request. 'Doubt it' he answered 'I'm looking to sleep.'

'Okay, hang the sign on the door then if you plan on sleeping, it'll keep the cleaners out of the room.'

'Got it, thanks.' He said and walked off with a wave.

His room was on the second floor and he found it easily and opened it with his key. It was smaller than the pictures on the website, but he accepted that was usually the case. He threw his luggage in the corner and pulled his toiletry bag out from the front slot. He brushed his teeth quickly, then stripped down to his boxers and climbed into bed. He laid awake for a minute or two, but not any longer, as weariness overcame him. The journey in was not really what he expected, but he felt that at last his troubles were behind him, at least for the moment. His last thoughts before sleep took him were not of prison cells, murder or death. They weren't even of Bernadette. After he shut his eyes, he thought only of the girl with dark hair on the stoop. Something about her was alluring and it was her image that was burned into his brain.

CHAPTER SIXTEEN

The hours faded by as Andrew's slumber continued. He'd wake periodically from a dream, but fall asleep again within moments, each dream dissolving into more sleep, no longer discernible from any other forgotten memory. When he woke for good, it was dark again. He'd passed an entire day under the sheets with his eyes shut, but strangely felt worse physically than he did before it, as if his body had grown accustomed to laying down and showed no interest in any other position.

It was hunger that finally forced him from his mattress. It attacked him fiercely, but only after he'd realized just how long he'd been out. He climbed out of bed begrudgingly and found refuge in a cold shower. He let the water pour down on his face for a quarter of an hour before he finally felt refreshed. The cold from the water eventually woke his limbs as the blood was shocked back into circulation, making him feel more awake both physically and mentally. He dug into his case and pulled out a pair of jeans and a shirt that he felt could be worn without ironing. His options were slim on that front considering his belongings had been shoved in a bag for over twenty-four hours at that stage.

He shaved after looking in the mirror and seeing a homeless guy staring back at him, then brushed his teeth to chase the dry cotton taste from his mouth. After getting ready, he grabbed his wallet and headed down to reception to get some information.

He used an ATM machine in the corner to withdraw some euros, then walked over to the front desk and greeted the same man he'd met that morning. 'You must be on a long shift.' He said as he approached.

'My relief phoned in sick. Glad to see you're up Mr. Dawson. The cleaning staff were worried you'd never let them in.'

'Yeah I was tired' Andrew said. 'Sorry, hope I didn't cause them any trouble.'

'Them, no. They're only afraid you'll not let them in only to complain later about not having fresh towels.'

'Is that right?'

'Well, either that or they were just afraid they might have to clean up after a dead guy. Either way, not to worry. What can I help you with? Planning on heading out?'

'I'm hungry. I could eat a horse. Can you recommend somewhere close to eat?'

The man looked over at the clock. Andrew followed his gaze. The hands showed it was nearing eleven pm. 'Wow, they really were probably worried' he thought, 'that's about seventeen hours.'

'There's usually plenty of places to eat, but it's pretty late and you might have missed the good places, they've probably stopped seating by now.'

'Oh, you got me wrong. I want something decent, but not looking for expensive anyhow. Is anyone open?

'You like kebabs?' he asked.

Andrew considered the question. 'Not sure I've ever even had one.'

'Do you eat chicken?'

'Yeah of course.'

'And garlic?'

'Uh . . . yes.'

'Then I'd guess you like kebabs. There's a place on the corner down the street.' He said and pointed in the direction across the street from the hotel. 'Order the chicken sheesh.'

'Thanks' Andrew said, 'I'll try it out.'

'I'd go now if I were you, then get out. If you wait much longer, you'll be the only sober fella in there.'

'Got it. Thanks again.'

Andrew walked down the front steps in the direction the man at reception pointed to. He crossed the street and disappeared around the corner. At the next corner, he caught a waft of meat and garlic and knew he was close. He saw the meat on a spit from the window and walked into the restaurant. The place was plenty busy, but not fully packed. Mostly, it was young men in suits with loosened or no ties. Andrew thought it must be the office workers in the area that flooded the surrounding streets, the after work crowd. Andrew walked to the counter and ordered the chicken sheesh as suggested. He paid and got a number from the clerk and was told to grab a seat and wait, which he did. The tables were heavy and wooden and the décor Mediterranean. Andrew took a seat near the back of the restaurant. He sat facing a mirror, which he instantly regretted, feeling strange enough by himself, he didn't need his own reflection for company. Part of him moving countries was in order to escape his past and he wasn't prepared to face the man in mirror quite yet. Not literally anyway. He got up from his chair and moved to the other side of the table, doing so as nonchalantly as possible. His number was called within minutes and he walked to the counter to pick up his food. When he got back to his table, he ate the food voraciously, as his hunger had grown greater each minute since waking. He finished the plate quickly and without once looking up. The food was delicious and he decided he'd done himself a disservice waiting so long to try a kebab. He felt self-conscious afterwards concerned that people saw him tear into his food like a starved hyena. When he finished and looked around at others sitting around enjoying their own dinners or engaged in conversation, he realized he might as well have been invisible. That was a welcomed change from the mean-eyed stares from strangers that filled his last few days at home. He sat slowly drinking his can of coke, people watching, happy once again to be a wall flower. Minutes after devouring his food, his brain finally registered the calories and he went from starved to very full and sleepy once again, despite his near marathon slumber.

He kept looking over at one particular group that sat talking loudly and laughing over their plates. Again it was a group of men in suits, though these gentlemen looked a few years older than most and wore more sophisticated attire. One or two even managed to keep their ties straight. There was a man at the edge of the table who Andrew thought looked very familiar. He looked to be in his thirties with dark hair that went slightly speckled with grey in places. He was engaging in the conversation, but appeared to be either more reserved than the others or at least looked preoccupied or distracted. Andrew guessed he was the boss from his demeanor. He appeared relaxed and amused, but not overly so. He conversed with the others, but let the louder ones do most of the talking, chiming in only once in a while for support. Plus, Andrew saw him walk over and pick up the check for the table. Something about the way he looked reminded Andrew of home, but he couldn't place him.

After the man returned from paying the bill, the others at the table all rose, gathered jackets and started to disperse. Most walked loudly by the table where Andrew sat finishing his coke and picked at the last one or two fries, including the man who looked familiar. He was the last to walk by and when he did, he paused in front of Andrew as he put on his jacket. Andrew was surprised when the man spoke to him, even more so when he realized the voice had a similar accent to his own. 'I saw you looking over, do you know some of my guys?'

'Me?' Andrew asked, 'No, sorry, I don't know any of them, I just got in yesterday.'

'Oh yeah, where from?' the man asked.

'I flew in from Boston.'

'Yeah, I was gonna say, I noticed your accent. You look familiar.' The man said. 'Where are you from?'

Andrew paused, not sure he was ready to relinquish his new found anonymity yet. He decided it wasn't worth hiding anything. 'Plus, what's one person.' He thought.

'I grew up in Quincy.' He said.

'No kidding' the man said 'me too.' and pulled out the chair across from Andrew. He started to sit down, but stopped and yelled over to his crowd of colleagues at the door first 'I'll catch up.'

'You mind if I sit? It's not often I run into people here from my hometown. Actually, this is the first time it's ever happened.'

'Really. You been here long?' Andrew asked.

'Over ten years, though it went by a lot faster than it sounds. I guess that's common.' The man sat across from Andrew and stared into his face. Andrew was unnerved by the man's gaze and continuous eye contact, but tried to hold his stare.

Finally, the man seemed to relax and lean back in his chair, crossing his leg over his knee. A hint of a smile came to his face as he seemed to ponder a question. He leaned forward on the table with his elbow keeping his leg crossed. Andrew found himself lean in as well in response.

The man asked in a low voice 'So what is it you're running from?'

Andrew was unsure how to respond. After a pause he asked 'What makes you think I'm running?'

'Well . . . you don't look happy enough to be on vacation. If you were, you'd probably not be alone and I'm pretty sure you wouldn't spend your first night eating dinner in this

147

place. Also, I don't see any maps on you or near you. Or, any other evidence of an itinerary for that matter. If you've lived here as long as I have you pick up on habits of American tourists. Believe me . . . they're usually smiling, carrying at least one map and for the most part mildly irritating'

'So, you drew your conclusion from that?' Andrew asked.

'Yes, mostly anyway. Plus, I can't remember the last time I watched someone eat alone in a restaurant without at least one glance at a mobile phone. You either don't have one on you or you're showing great will power. I've assumed you don't have one. And what young man doesn't have a cell phone these days? My guess is it's really only those that don't want to be in contact with anyone they knew before today. How am I doing? Getting warmer at least?'

'So, I have to be running away from something?'

'Or running towards something. But in the end, what's the fucking difference if we're all running to the same place.'

'Okay, okay' Andrew said admitting defeat. 'Let's say I'm running from something. But, to be honest, I'm not ready to talk about it.'

'Naturally. If you were, you wouldn't be running.'

Andrew shrugged. 'True I guess.'

'Hey listen, I'm just busting your chops. Believe me

brother, you're not the first yank with problems to jump on an Aer Lingus jet and believe he's flying those green wings to Eden. Shit, there's two sitting at this table.' He said and laughed lightly. The man got up from the chair slowly and stood up straight, stretching his arms out then shaking them out by his side.

He was as tall as Andrew and as broad, but he carried a few more years around the waist. 'It was good talking to you anyway bud. You planning on sticking around for a while.' The man asked.

'That's the plan' Andrew answered 'But so far, that's the extent of it.'

'So you're looking for work then?'

'Yes actually, though I haven't started looking yet.'

'What did you do back home?'

'A carpenter.' Andrew answered.

'You and everyone else. I think you might have missed the boat on that here I'm afraid, those jobs disappeared when the Celtic Tiger took his catnap. Can you do anything else?'

Andrew held up his hands. 'I'll shovel shit against the tide if it means I get a fresh start.'

The man laughed hard and slapped the table. 'Good! I like to hear it.' He reached into his inside jacket pocket and pulled out a pen. Then he took out his wallet and pulled out a business card. He flipped it to the blank side and dropped it on the table and began writing. 'A friend of mine owns a restaurant close by here. He owes me. Go see him and tell him I sent you. It's just up the street past Stephen's Green.' He slid his card across the table. Andrew picked it up and read the handwritten name on the back. It read 'Dawson Street Grille'. He laughed.

'What's funny?' the man asked.

'Not funny just coincidental. My name is Dawson. Andrew Dawson.'

The man paused and gave him a look with squinted eyes. 'That is funny Dawson. Maybe it was meant to be.' He held out his hand across the table. 'My name and number are on the back. Give me a call if there's any issues or you can't get a hold of the owner, his name's Donal Coughlin.'

Andrew stood and took the man's hand and shook it. 'Thanks. Wow, man, I really appreciate it. Okay, Donal Coughlin, I'll remember that.'

'Nice to meet you Andrew. My name's Danny Carson. Go see Donal. Oh, and don't fuck it up.' With a smirk he took his hand back. Andrew watched him walk out and leave a tip in a jar by the register, then disappear from view out the front door.

As soon as the man said his name, Andrew's brain kicked in. 'That's why he's so familiar' he thought. He had seen

Danny Carson before, likely met him at some stage in his life. He was around the same age as Andrew's brother and from the same neighborhood. He knew of him anyway. There was some mystery attached to Danny Carson, which he added to by apparently never returning to the Boston area. His reputation was that of a really good person, but dangerous to cross. Like Andrew, Carson had lost a brother. The difference was that Carson's brother was killed. Within a couple years after that, the people involved in his murder, which occurred during a robbery of the younger Carson's restaurant, started disappearing. Danny Carson's name was thrown around as a suspect. Whether he did it or not, his absence from Quincy ever since added to the mystique. 'I'll have to play this pretty close' Andrew thought 'Real close.'

CHAPTER SEVENTEEN

Andrew figured there was no point in waiting to check out Dawson Street Grille. The sooner he found work, the better off he'd be, no matter what it was. His savings would only last him a short while, especially with the exchange rate and incurring cross border fees. He headed up towards Saint Stephen's Green the next morning after a light breakfast. A girl working at reception in the hotel was able to explain to him the directions, which were straightforward, walk to Grafton Street, take a right, then take a left. The walk took him less than ten minutes. He arrived at the restaurant, which was part of a strand of bars and restaurants that spanned a few blocks on Dawson Street. Unfortunately, the place wasn't opened when he showed up. He peered through the window to see if there was staff inside preparing, but could see no one. There was a menu on a pedestal just inside the door and he could make out from where he stood that there was a lunch section. That was promising, since he'd only have to occupy himself for a few hours before anyone showed up.

He walked around for a while getting his bearings in the daylight finally. He walked a loop around Dawson and back up Grafton Street then crossed into the Green, which he did a lap through. He thought Grafton Street was pleasant at first, but it grew nerve wracking trying to get through the packs of tourists crowding around various street performers and buskers, each ranging in skill, most were either just okay or awful. That didn't seem to matter however as crowds gathered regardless of the performance quality. After he finished his walk through the Green, he found a pharmacy for a few essentials. Also, he found a phone shop and bought the cheapest smart phone off the rack and picked up a prepaid sim card. He figured as someone hunting for a job he needed a better contact method then saying 'call my cheap hotel and ask for my room.' He wasn't even sure if his room had a phone in it. He assumed it had one, but it never occurred to him to check and he hadn't noticed if it did or not.

After his walk and his shopping, he went into a small internet cafe and paid the man running it two euros to use a slow, old computer to check his email. He checked his account, but it was nothing but junk mail. He wanted to check Facebook, but he had closed his account the second he was able to after his acquittal. He opted for his own sanity not to scroll through the various comments that were venomously splattered across his homepage. Suffice to say when he got out, he had a fraction the number of friends he had the day he went in, both real and virtual. With no social media to peruse and an unwillingness to read any Boston online newspaper, he spent most of the remaining twenty minutes he purchased to read up on the menu of the Dawson Street Grille. 'At least I will have appeared to do some research' he thought. He did a search for the restaurant name and found they had a website. He clicked on the link and brought up the page. He scrolled through some of the reviews on the side, they were all glowing, but what else could be expected from the restaurant's own webpage. He clicked into the 'contact us' section. He found the breakdown of serving times above the frequently asked questions section. They opened for lunch daily at one o'clock until four, then served dinner from five thirty until eleven. He thought if they opened at one for lunch, then it was nearing the time the staff would likely have to be in. He only had a few minutes left on the computer's timer and opened up the a la carte menu section. It opened in a pdf and he scrolled down the list, first starters, then a grill section, then seafood. The list of food looked a cut above what he was used to, both from a quality and price perspective. He guessed he probably heard of about fifty percent of the items included in the dinner menu. He had actually tasted probably closer to thirty percent. He read through the rest of the menus and finished just before the timer ran out and his computer went on standby.

He picked up his shopping bag and headed back out onto the street towards the restaurant. It was still not one o'clock, but he figured he'd get more attention if he showed up before opening hours anyhow. The front door was closed and the menu pedestal was still inside the door, but when he tried the handle it opened and he walked into the room. The ceilings inside were taller than he expected and it made the restaurant quite airy. There were different pieces of art, mostly paintings, hanging on the wall. The tables were wooden and looked heavy and expensive. Several tables lined the middle of the dining area and there were elevated sections with round leather booths that appeared to be areas for pre-booked groups. Andrew could hear music from somewhere. He guessed it was coming from the kitchen as the staff prepared for lunch and prepped for the later dinner service. He walked deeper into the room and called out 'Hello?' Hoping to get someone's attention.

He was startled to hear a man's voice answer from behind him. 'How's it going? Help you with something?' it said.

Andrew turned around and saw a man sitting at a low

table near the entrance. He was going through some papers that were spread out on the table itself. He must've walked right by the man when he entered. 'Hi, sorry, I didn't see you there.' He said. 'I'm looking for Donal. I believe he's the owner or manager.'

The man stopped sifting through his paperwork and pulled down his glasses from his eyes and looked over at Andrew. Andrew put him at or around forty five or fifty years old.

'I'm Donal.' He said and picked up the papers he had across the table and stacked them into a neater pile. 'What can I do for you?'

'Um, Danny Carson sent me up. He mentioned you might have some work for me. I'm new to the area.'

'Danny sent you huh? Okay, here sit down.' He said and kicked out the chair across from him so Andrew could take a seat, which he did.

'What are you looking to do?' Donal asked.

'Really anything sir. I just flew in a couple nights ago from Boston. I've moved over here and I'm trying to settle in. I'm willing to take on anything you've got for work.'

'Okay, have you waited tables before?' he asked.

'No sir, I haven't.' Andrew replied.

'Alright, what about worked in a bar, either serving or assisting?'

'No, sorry, I'm afraid not.'

'Okay, so then . . . have you worked in a restaurant ever before in your life? Washing dishes even?'

'Uh . . . No I haven't.' Andrew answered. He was beginning to feel that this was a dead end.

Donal put his hand to his face for a minute. He shook his head after a few seconds and said to himself, 'Fucking Danny.'

'Listen sir, it's safe to say, I have very little experience working in a restaurant. In fact, I have none. Probably the closest I've come to working in a restaurant is actually eating in one. And, I must say, I'm not sure I've eaten in one this nice ever.' Andrew said.

Donal didn't say anything. He just smiled and shook his head.

Andrew continued talking to plead his case, 'I don't mean to offend, but when I met Danny yesterday, he seemed pretty confident you'd find something for me. Should I have taken him with a grain of salt? Is there nothing for me here?'

Donal stopped and considered his response. 'There's plenty of shit I could have you do, sure. It would just make my life easier if you'd done any of them before. Danny sent you, so I'll put you to work. Wouldn't be the first time he sent me an employee so green he had roots. How do you know Danny anyway?'

'I don't I guess.' Andrew answered. 'I met him randomly yesterday for the first time. We're from the same neighborhood though.'

Donal nodded his head. 'I don't think Danny Carson meets anyone randomly, but anyway, we'll get you doing something. What's your name?'

'My name's Andrew. Andrew Dawson.'

'Dawson is it? Well you're in the right spot then. Okay Andrew Dawson, when can you start working?'

Andrew looked around before he answered, 'I can start right this second.'

Donal put his hands up in a slowdown gesture. 'Listen, why don't you come back tonight at half five. I'll be here, so just come in and ask for me if I'm not out front. I'll see if I can think of what to do with you between now and then. Sound alright?'

'Yes it does, it sounds great, thanks Donal. I really appreciate it. Do I need anything with me?'

'If you have a black t shirt or something close to it, just wear that and a pair of jeans. That's basically the uniform here. Other than that, we'll see you later on.'

'Black t shirt and jeans, got it.' Andrew said. He got up and tucked the chair back under the table. While standing with his hands gripping the chair he said 'Danny said you owed him a favor. Must have been some favor he did for you.'

Donal looked up from the table at Andrew as he put his reading glasses back on. 'You could say that I guess. It's no secret, this place is his favor to me. He invested in the restaurant.'

'Oh okay, so he's like a silent partner.' Andrew asked.

Donal shrugged, 'Loudest silent partner I've ever known, but yes, I guess you could say that.'

Andrew nodded his head. He let go of the chair and stood up straight. 'I'll be back this afternoon, five thirty. Thank you again.'

'See you then Andrew. Don't mention it.' Donal waved him goodbye as Andrew weaved through the tables in the dining room and left the restaurant.

CHAPTER EIGHTEEN

A black t shirt was easy to come by. Andrew found one for basically no money in a store inside the shopping center at Stephen's Green. Jeans were more difficult to find. They seemed to be sized differently than in America and he wasted more time than he planned trying to find a pair that fit him right. Finally happy that he had his uniform sorted out, he walked back to the same internet café he was in before. This time he paid the man five euros and was granted an hour on the computer. Now that he had a job on the horizon at least, he had to get serious about finding a place to live. There seemed to be one or two websites that were pretty good and he searched through a number of places. His plan was to stay as close to the city center as possible for as cheap as possible. A few places looked right for him and he sent off requests to the contacts by email. He printed off those apartments plus a few others and took them with him back to the hotel.

He still had time to kill when he got back upstairs to his

hotel room so he pulled his running sneakers from his bag along with a pair of shorts. He asked at reception if there was any decent routes for jogging around the hotel, but the girl working the desk gave no real insight. She mentioned a canal down the street that he could run beside and at least then not lose his way back. It seemed a reasonable suggestion, so he headed south for it and found it minutes later. He turned west and ran alongside the canal. He felt good to be doing something active, but the route wasn't great and several times he needed to stop before crossing the street. The road along the canal was packed with cars and cyclists. The cars were barely moving with the traffic. He was surprised at how aggressive the cyclists were on their small path. Most seemed to pedal without regard for danger. He ran for a couple miles he judged. The further west he ran, the dingier the surroundings seemed to grow. When he reached a set of flats that looked too much like the projects in South Boston, he turned and began his jog back.

The canal wasn't a great running route, but the receptionist was on to something since he found his way back to the hotel without any hesitation. He took a shower and got ready to go back to the restaurant. He double and triple checked his t shirt and jeans for hidden tags in the mirror then started back up the street. He was a little early and slowed his pace and took a short detour through the

Green before walking down Dawson Street. He kept a close eye on the clock on his new phone and at twenty minutes past five he decided it was reasonably early to arrive.

He walked in to a much busier place than he'd seen earlier that day. There seemed to be a full wait staff dressed and ready. There were four of them that he could see, walking around the dining room cleaning off tables and straightening chairs and table ornaments preparing for the dinner crowd. Donal walked out through the kitchen. He saw Andrew right away and waved him over. Andrew crossed the dining room and joined Donal outside the door to the kitchen. They shook hands once again. Donal said, 'let me show you around quickly and introduce you to a few people.'

'Sounds good.' Andrew answered. He followed Donal into the back. The kitchen was smaller than he expected, not that he'd spent time in any restaurant kitchens before, but he still pictured it bigger. It was hot back there, and it was loud. He could hear fans going, music playing and a lot of banging noises coming from somewhere. They walked around a corner and he could see the entire place. It was a rectangular room, separated by a counter in the middle, making it look like two chicken runs. There were stoves in each area and the center seemed to be the prep area and looked to have refrigerators underneath the counter. There were three people steadily working away at different things. One looked to be putting garnishes into silver pots and placing them into slots within the counter. Another was rough chopping vegetables for a soup.

'I don't want to get in the guys' way here, so I won't walk you through. This is the kitchen staff, 'hey guys!' he yelled. The kitchen staff looked up. 'This is Andrew. He's starting work with us tonight. When you're done prepping, introduce yourself to him.' They nodded in unison at the request.

'Here' Donal said 'Follow me, I think the Chef is around here somewhere. Usually he goes over the menu with the wait staff one by one to make sure they're clear on everything on there.' He continued walking. Andrew followed along nodding his head. They entered a smaller room that housed dry goods. Donal paused and looked back at Andrew, 'We do one or two specials usually per night that change quite a bit. Oh, and fair warning, Chefs can be temperamental in my experience. Our's is no different. Poor Ivan thinks he's an artist sometimes, so he gets moody about certain things. His favorite things to bitch about are well-done steaks and pretty much any changes requested from what's on the menu. Just stay out of his way when he has his period and you'll be fine.' Donal looked at Andrew. He looked down at his feet, then up across his shoulders.

'Plus, you're a big enough guy that he probably won't say a thing to you. He's more the type to bitch at those that can't physically intimidate him. Ask the waitresses about him, I'm sure they each have a horror story or two.'

'Great. Okay, think I'll just stay out of his way to be safe.' Andrew answered.

There was a large walk-in freezer and refrigerator out the back that Donal pointed out. Then he opened a door that had a set of steps that led up to a second level. 'Up there we keep a lot of the business files, some other paper supplies, shit like that. If you can't find me I'm usually up there trying to reconcile credit card receipts with the night's intake or trying to figure out which employee might be skimming off the top. Ivan and the others go up there to type up the specials and print the inserts out for the menus.' Donal craned his neck up the stairway, 'Ivan, you up there?' he yelled.

Andrew heard a voice yell down. 'Coming down now.' It said and Andrew could hear heavy footsteps walking down the stairs. Seconds later, Ivan got to the bottom of the steps and joined the two men in the hall. 'Ivan, this is Andrew, he's gonna be working here starting tonight.'

Andrew held out his hand and Ivan took it. He wasn't quite six feet, but he was close. He had dark hair, but it was buzzed down close to his head. He wore a five o'clock shadow that Andrew took for European designer stubble and he was much thinner than Andrew thought any chef should be. 'Nice to meet you' Andrew said.

Ivan looked down at Andrew's hand, then followed his arm with his eyes up to Andrew's shoulder. 'What, do we need security now?' he asked.

'Funny Ivan.' Donal said, 'if anyone does here, it's you, so keep young Andrew here on side would ya?'

'Welcome.' Ivan said and took his hand back from Andrew'. 'Ask me any questions about the menu. It's better you know from me, not these others.' He said flailing his hand out towards the dining room to indicate anyone else that worked there besides himself Andrew guessed.

'Will do. Thanks Ivan.'

'You're welcome.' Ivan said, then nodded and walked off into the kitchen.

Andrew looked at Donal and said, 'seems alright.'

'Ah, he's alright. Great in the kitchen anyway. Ivan's from Budapest. A couple drinks after dinner service and he'll be telling you how the best Palinka in Hungary is from his hometown and listing off Nobel Prize winners and famous inventors from Hungary, just wait for it. The first time it's interesting. It grows less so every time after that. But, you wait until goulash or goose leg is on the special board and for fucksake, you'll fall in love with the man.'

Andrew laughed. 'I'll keep an eye out for it then, great.'

'Okay Andrew, that's pretty much it back here. Let's head out to the dining room.'

Andrew nodded and followed Donal after he started walking out. They walked back through the kitchen area and out the same door into the dining room. Leaving the kitchen was a relief and Andrew could feel the sweat on his torso. He got a chill from it when they were back out in the dining room. 'So, Donal?' he asked.

'Yup' Donal said and stopped walking.

'I'm just wondering. What are your plans? I mean, what do you think you'll have me do tonight?'

'Oh right, okay. Well, I've been short on wait staff recently, so I'd like you to learn to wait tables. But to let you run out there on your own tonight would probably lose me more money than anything else . . . no offense.'

Andrew shook his head. 'None taken.'

'Good. So, I want to get one of the girls to train you as a waiter. You'll have to do some busing of tables and clean up stuff as well, but for the most part tonight you'll stick with Vicky. She's one of the waitresses here. She'll show you what to do, you know, let you take orders from tables, tell you what you did wrong. Shit like that. That alright?'

'Yeah, great, perfect. Like I said, whatever you need.'

A girl walked out of the door carrying a tray of small

candles that she started putting on each table. 'Ah, there's Vicky there.' Donal said. 'Vicky! Come over here a second.'

The girl left the tray on a table and walked over to where Donal and Andrew stood talking. She had dark hair that was somewhere between wavy and curly. Her skin was white and unblemished. She wore dark eyeliner and had thick lashes that covered eyes that looked royal blue in the light. Andrew thought they were so blue they had to be fake. 'Hi' he said and held out his hand.

She took his hand lightly and shook it once. 'Hi.' Andrew squinted slightly and suddenly recognized the girl. She had almost knocked him down the stairs the morning he arrived at the hotel. He wondered if she recognized him, but didn't want to bring it up. 'I'm Andrew.' He said.

'Vicky' she answered. They stood in silence for a few seconds until Donal broke up the moment. 'Okay, Vicky, like I explained earlier, can you show Andrew the ropes tonight.'

'Yeah okay sure.' She said.

'Alright then, I'll leave you to it, I've got work to do myself now believe it or not. Andrew you're in good hands. Vicky's another of Danny Carson's blow-ins. She came in as green as you and now she's the best I've got.'

'Aren't you sweet?' she said to Donal

'I try to be. Okay Andrew, good luck.'

'Okay, great.' Andrew said, 'thanks Donal.'

When Donal walked away Andrew turned back towards Vicky. 'So . . . where can I start?' he asked. In response she walked over to where she left the tray of candles and carried it over to Andrew then stuck it into his hands. It was heavier than expected and he had to adjust his balance quickly so that he didn't drop it. 'Here' she said. 'Start by holding these.'

When he regained control over the wobbly tray he answered. 'no problem' and followed behind her as she walked into the dining room.

CHAPTER NINETEEN

'What's Ranelagh like? Is it better than like Rathgar or Terenure?' Andrew asked the man working reception at the hotel. After days of exchanging banter, Andrew grew to like the man called George who seemed to work nonstop at the hotel.

'Ranelagh, Rathgar, Terenure, Rathmines, they're all grand villages. It depends what you're looking for. Ranelagh's the closest. You could probably kick a football to it from here. It's probably considered the most posh too, besides Ballsbridge or Donnybrook. They're all nice. I'd say you're fine with any of them, just stay clear of places like Inichicore and Dolphin's Barn.' George answered.

'Why does Dolphin's Barn sound familiar? I can picture the name for some reason, I must have past it at some stage.'

'I don't know. It's a straight shot west down the Canal, it's not too far from here. It's not the worst, but there's a lot of flats around there that's all. They can be rough.'

'Flats? You mean like what I'd call projects right?'

'I think so, close enough anyway.'

'Ah, okay, I know why I know it. I took a jog down the Canal and must have made it down the far. I remember seeing the flats and then I turned around.'

'Probably the right move.'

'I thought it was at the time.'

'So you're going to view this place in Ranelagh then?' George asked pointing to one of the printouts that Andrew laid on the counter.'

'Yeah, well there's two places in Ranelagh. I'm gonna see 'em both this morning and get it out of the way. Are they walking distance?'

'You could take the Luas if you're lazy, but yeah, it's probably a ten to fifteen minute walk at most. This first one' he slide the print out in front of Andrew, 'that's on Ranelagh road. So you're literally walking down to the Canal, crossing the street and it's on that road. The other one is a little further down. If you walk to the village and turn right at the Triangle, its right by there, you can't miss it.'

'Thanks George' Andrew said 'Appreciate the help once again.'

'Don't mention it. Add a nice review on tripadvisor or something.' He said smiling. 'I'd hope for the same if I was ever moving to Boston.'

'I think you'd find that in Boston, there's still plenty of

first generation Irish. You'd probably know more people there than I would.'

'I've had friends that had been over. Maybe I'll check it out at some stage.'

'You should, definitely.' Andrew said, then thought to himself, 'Just don't tell anyone you know me.'

'Alright George' he said and folded up the printouts and put them into his pocket. 'I better go check these places out. Gotta work again later on.'

'Good luck Andrew.' George said.

Andrew left in the direction that George had sent him. The small hotel had grown on him in the few days he stayed there. He attributed this to the friendly familiarity that the staff showed towards him. He'd miss having someone come in and clean up after him every day too. He knew it wasn't economical for him to stay there any longer than he had to. If he was really going to give his fresh start his best effort, he couldn't live like he was on vacation. Plus, he wanted to feel settled, and hoped an apartment would help do that. Only a few days away from home and he already was beginning to feel free again. He hoped a few more weeks and he'd feel close to normal, if that would ever be possible. Things had happened that he couldn't just forget. He had been accused and arrested for murder. He was sure that's a memory that wouldn't go away easily. It was only a short time ago and he felt the ghost of that memory linger between him and any person he met for the first time. Always in the back of his mind, 'What happens if this person hears what I had allegedly done? Will they believe me or will they run like hell?' The inevitable coming out of those skeletons haunted him, never more so than the previous night as he followed Vicky around, making small talk as she walked him through how to do his new job. He liked her. He liked everyone he'd met there. Would they see him any differently if they knew?

He spent so much energy worrying about getting on with his own life, he felt selfish every time he climbed out of his own self-centered well and remembered that as far as victims go, he got off the easiest. The count was up to four girls now that were dealt a much more punishing and final fate than him. These were four young women that were innocent. He had gone to school with them, had known two of them well enough to call them friends. Now they were gone. Whoever dealt them that fate was still in the wind. With that perspective, he'd gotten off light. 'It should be Gina O'Neil and Lisa Stark that occupy my mind.' He thought, 'Not my own fractured shadow.' Fear gripped him with the realization that there could be more. There were only four girls that had been found. 'Also, what's to stop the real killer from doing it again? He's free, there's no incentive to stop now. If anything, he probably feels more in control.'

Andrew shook the thoughts to the back of his head as he approached a building that housed the address on his printout. He pulled out the form from his pocket to double check the apartment number and rang the doorbell. A second later, he heard a buzzing noise and he pushed the large door forward. The buzz and click sounds reminded him of the prison. He pushed the memory away. The door opened into the hall and he walked in. The ceilings were high and a set of cement steps lay in front of him. The lighting was poor as the surrounding walls had no windows and therefore no natural light. On the wall a bulletin board was hung and cluttered with pieces of papers that varied from pizza delivery menus, trash day reminders and phone numbers of house cleaners that could be hired by the hour.

A dingy carpet covered much of the painted cement floor. It was discolored in many random places and worn heavily in a line leading to the stairs. The apartment for rent was on the first floor. Andrew looked around for the right apartment door number and found it behind a heavy fire proof door that snapped shut loudly behind him after he walked into a smaller, darker hallway. The inner hall gave him an eerie tingle down his spine. He didn't envy the late night fast food delivery man, having to spend many evenings knocking on doors in these claustrophobic hallways.

He knocked on the apartment door and a man in his sixty's or seventy's answered and let him in. The man was gruff and seemed put out by the visit as if Andrew was intruding. 'Not exactly a sales man.' Andrew thought. The apartment was unappealing. It had large windows that let in plenty of light, though much of it struggled to penetrate an ageless layer of grime on the glass, giving the room a speckled, hazy effect. This ended up being the apartment's best feature. The rooms were untidy and the carpet in the apartment was more worn and spot-laden than that in the main hall. The heating system consisted of two storage heaters, one in a corner in the sitting room, the other in the bedroom, which Andrew was informed often didn't work very well and smelled of burning hair when it did. The kitchen was the smallest he'd ever seen, but mostly it was the layer of grease around the stove top that turned him off it. Within thirty seconds, he knew the place was not for him and every second after that he had to hold back the urge to run out of there. Some ingrained respect for his elders made him continue to be courteous despite not receiving the same in return. He was glad to leave minutes later and headed off down the street, feeling dirty for having spent longer than a minute inside that dump.

He was slightly discouraged, but only because his hopes

had been so high going in. When he reached the second viewing, his expectations had level set to reality. The lowered expectations served him better and the second apartment on the whole, though more snug, was much nicer. It had clean floors and was freshly painted. The windows could be seen through, which was what he'd grown to expect from glass. The sitting room was smaller, but the furniture looked relatively new and comfortable. The apartment had a kitchenette as opposed to a kitchen, but at a glance there were no obvious signs of aged grease stuck to the countertop around the stove. Best of all, he could picture himself living there. He told the owner as much and said that he'd take it. The owner seemed glad to give it to him and promised to draw up the lease provided Andrew could get Donal to confirm his employment and pick up a bank draft for a deposit. They exchanged numbers and shook hands.

Andrew felt lighter leaving there and walked back up the street towards his hotel feeling he had accomplished something that morning. He looked forward to getting his own place and hoped to have it secured in the next couple of days. Moving across the Atlantic had always seemed daunting to him, but within a week he had a job secured, in a stalled economy no less, and now was close to having a place to live. Never an optimist, he still felt a nugget of caution looming in his stomach. But for the moment, for the night at least, he was going to consider the day a success. 'Now, to buy a few more black t shirts so I can be clean going to work.' He thought and headed past the hotel and up to the shops on Grafton Street.

CHAPTER TWENTY

Andrew walked out of the kitchen carrying three hot dinner plates the way that Vicky showed him. One was in his left hand which he held with three fingers underneath, then his pinky and thumb extended to balance another on top, braced on his forearm. His right hand grasped the remaining plate tightly and he kept it close to his left in case he needed to use it to regain balance. His forearm stung with pain from the hot plate resting on top of it. No one else working the tables seemed to notice, apparently anyone with more than six months experience working in a restaurant grew impervious to burns. At two days, he wasn't yet and he noticed his forearm was red raw when he looked at it after he delivered the plates to the table across the dining room. He shook it out as he walked. He headed out back to see if there were more plates to go out.

'Ivan's looking for you.' Vicky said as she breezed past him carrying plates of food to another table. Andrew was walking that way anyhow and ventured back into the kitchen. He stood on the edge where the wait staff dropped off order slips. He could feel the heat from the kitchen as soon as he walked in from the dining room. With the stoves on full blast, the room was hotter than a crematorium. The kitchen staff were all required to wear hats specially made to absorb sweat from the forehead. They had a rotating break system during the night to make sure each had the opportunity to cool down for three to five minutes at a time during the evening rush. Everyone took the breaks except for Ivan. Andrew figured it was time spent in that heat that was likely why the man was as thin as he was. He manned the kitchen at all times and was very hands on. Donal had mentioned to Andrew that Ivan thought himself an artist. After watching him work only twice, Andrew had to agree. He was a perfectionist and could be temperamental, but he appeared to work harder than anyone Andrew had met before. Also, he seemed to truly love what he did for a living. 'Ivan!' Andrew yelled over the noise of the active kitchen. Ivan looked up, saw Andrew and pointed for him to walk around the back. Andrew did and Ivan went around the other way so as to not cross through the kitchen. He had two slips in his hand, which he roughly shoved into Andrew's palm. 'Young Andrew' he said. 'There's no temp on the ribeye for the first one and I can't read your hand writing on the other. I need you to do better.' He stood looking Andrew in the eye. He didn't appear angry, just really matter of fact.

Andrew looked at the slips, then back at Ivan. The man was right. Andrew's hand writing was atrocious. It was barely legible even to himself as he tried to read it back. He'd hardly hand written anything since he was in school. Many restaurants had wait staff carry tablets that relay orders directly to the kitchen. Dawson Street Grille wasn't quite there yet. Pen and paper remained the communication medium. Pens were like gold dust around there. Each waiter had his or her own stash. The slips were sequentially numbered and handed out by Donal at the beginning of each night. He had to write neater, that was obvious. Forgetting the steak's temperature was just an oversight, a rookie mistake. He looked back up at Ivan's face.

'Okay?' Ivan said. 'You bring them right back.' He said and pointed to the slips in Andrew's hand.

'Yes sir.' Andrew said. 'Sorry Ivan.'

'No time for sorry Andrew, too busy. Just do better next time.' Ivan said and started back around to the busy kitchen.

'Will do.' Andrew said and headed back to the dining room. He confirmed the steak order and sent that slip back into the kitchen, then rewrote the other in a neater hand. He looked at the clock, wrote the time down on the slip and yelled 'Fire it!' That was the system for letting the kitchen know to get the main courses started. Vicky told him you had to judge the table to know when to fire an order. A group that gathered to have drinks and talk, might want to take their time. So there was no point in firing that main course until everyone finished with their appetizers. It was the booze that made the money really, so it was worth letting a table linger that had the drinks flowing. Other tables may have two people on a first date and the conversation might look slow and awkward. If they're flying through their appetizers or salad, then it was wise to fire it as soon as you got back to the kitchen after dropping off the starters. Judging the tables like this proved difficult to Andrew on the first night when Vicky was testing him and making a game out of it. On his second night, it was nearly impossible for him as the staff was short-handed so he handled quite a few tables alone. His timing was off at least a few times. He hoped no one really noticed, but they likely did.

Donal was there greeting people at the door and seating them at tables. There was a small bar and waiting area by the front entrance, he could usually be found around there talking to some of the regulars that came in for dinner, but had a drink first. There were also several regulars that seemed to arrive later in the evening just for drinks.

Donal approached him a couple times earlier in the night to make sure he was doing alright. 'You managing?' he'd asked a few times.

Andrew didn't want to appear overwhelmed, so he always responded something like, 'yeah boss, I'm doing alright.' They both knew he was struggling, but when there was a lull after the seven o'clock crowd finished up before the later crowd came in, Donal chatted to him for a few minutes and let him know he was doing okay and told him not to get too stressed. 'You're brand new he said. 'Don't get too stressed. I expect a few mistakes. You'll get it soon.'

The other wait staff pitched in and helped him out whenever possible. A few times he'd hustle to the kitchen to pick up plates only to find one of the others had already run the food out to the tables. The same would happen when he'd remember he hadn't bussed a table or dropped dessert menus off or refreshed a round of drinks. 'That's not because you're new' Vicky had told him, 'That's just something we all do to help each other out.'

It was all new to him really. He worked the last decade or so on building sites or doing home renovations. Those days were typically long with frequent lulls in activity, especially as an apprentice when his lack of knowledge and experience meant he couldn't do anything on his own. He had to move at the pace the journeyman set and that varied depending on who it was and how ambitious they were. Two nights in the restaurant and doing nothing was not an option. Everyone had to be moving. They were either taking orders, dropping off food, carrying drinks, dropping checks or cleaning. Cleaning seemed to be constant and it was something Donal seemed to take seriously. 'People don't come here to eat from a trough' was a line he'd already used at least five times in two nights. Andrew found the evenings flew by and it was all down to pace. After two nights, he decided that for the moment at least, he really enjoyed the pace. He could just work. He needed to be organized and to learn what he was doing, but it seemed from observing the others, that once those basics were down, it was all experience and reaction. Concious thought barely seemed to come into it when the entire restaurant was moving at the speed of light.

He liked the comradery that the restaurant seemed to offer as well. The place was busy and Donal wanted every customer taken care of like they were the only ones there eating. It took everyone there working together to make that happen. Every person there, from the bus boy to the head chef had a role to play to meet that ultimate end. Each had to give it their best effort and pitch in beyond their own role when needed. That's what Donal wanted and so that's what he rewarded. He saw restaurants as not just a place to eat good food, but as a place to meet people, socialize and enjoy good food and surroundings. He told Andrew on his first night, that the food was very important. But, if the food was really good and the service or atmosphere was shit, then most people these days wouldn't bother coming back. There were too many options, so to stay competitive, they had to focus on getting the full package right. In that spirit, any and all tips were pooled between the wait staff and the bartender, bus boys and kitchen staff were all tipped out at the end of the night.

Once the final dinner orders were out and most of the checks dropped and paid for, the restaurant became a different place. It went from hectic and breakneck speed to one of relaxation. As everyone pitched in to clean up and finish up any last dessert or drink orders the kitchen staff would throw on some kind of snack for the staff, usually pizza's or calamari. Donal went around to each of the staff and took the staff drink order, the first one at the end of shift was on the house.

Andrew really enjoyed this part of the night. In his first two shifts, he didn't say much. He just listened to a lot of the joking back and forth between some of the other staff and sipped his beer slowly. Finishing the night's service made them feel like they collectively accomplished something. At least that was the impression Andrew got those first two nights. He'd heard they'd often head out after work and go for a few drinks, but he was happy enough for the time being to enjoy his staff drink, then head back to his room. Both nights he walked back to the hotel by himself. Hustling from the service worked up a sweat and left him too wired to go to bed, so he took his time each night walking back, taking in the surroundings including the cool spring air. The refreshing air cooled him off on his walk and dialed his engine down, so that both of his first two nights after working he fell into bed and slept a comfortable, dreamless sleep.

CHAPTER TWENTY-ONE

Over a month past in front of Andrew's eyes in a blur. A month into his journey and he still felt that he'd only just arrived in Dublin. Day after day flew by, it was as if time ticked away in the background without him having any perception of its passing. His month in Dublin felt half as long as his few days locked in a Massachusetts prison. 'That's likely part of the punishment' he guessed. Time was supposed to crawl by slowly inside prison. Most new things he encountered thus far had occurred within that first week, including a new job, new friends and coworkers and a new apartment. After that first week, where he felt things were hectic despite being energized by its speed, a routine began to develop. He wasn't exactly sure, but he guessed he had worked twenty five or twenty six out of thirty days at the restaurant since arriving in the country. There was a span of two straight weeks were he couldn't recall if he'd taken a day off. He liked it that way at the minute. Perhaps that pace wasn't sustainable and it probably wasn't healthy either given the late night drinks and food after closing hours, but he believed it kept him focused and sane at least in the first month in Dublin. He enjoyed the job. He liked the work and going to work each afternoon or evening became more part of his social life than a nine to five job every could.

He'd settled into his new place as well. Only days after his viewing, he found himself unpacking his one large suitcase full of belongings in his new apartment. The area where he rented grew on him quickly because of its convenience to the city center and its local amenities. The village seemed to be full of people always, even when walking home late at night after a shift. There was something comforting about that to Andrew, like the presence of others made the night less threatening.

The downside was however, whenever he looked himself in the mirror, guilt ate at him. He'd been there a month and still hadn't even contacted his mother, never mind go to see her. Each day he'd wake up and say to himself, 'today's the day' only to find a reason shortly after to put it off. There was something holding him back, but he didn't know what. He wanted to see her. He missed her badly. But, some unseen barrier still existed. And for that, he felt guilty, which was yet another reason just to bury himself in his work.

Each shift at the restaurant came with incremental

improvement in his work. He became more comfortable and his mistakes grew less frequent. He noticed a corresponding rise in his tips, which steadily began to increase with each passing day. The people working at the restaurant seemed to accept him pretty quickly into their fold. Within the first week, he thought they lightened towards him on the whole and Andrew responded by trying to be more open with them. He chipped in with the workplace banter whenever he could, though he was still pretty shy about it and was careful not to cross the line with anyone he didn't have a good read on yet. A few times in the last couple weeks, he'd even tagged along for a couple drinks after work. He felt awkward doing so at first, but the others often insisted and made sure he felt welcome when he joined. Still, despite all that, he kept a large part of himself reserved. He believed he had developed a good relationship with Donal. It was easy to do so because Donal was genuinely a nice person. Plus, each time he watched him diffuse a conflict or just do something hands-on to manage his people, his level of respect for the man increased. Also, he kept close to Vicky whenever he could. Out of everyone, she talked to him the most and seemed to be the most tolerant of his incompetence at the beginning. He knew a fondness for her was slowly building within him. He wasn't sure he was ready for anything like that or if she even looked at him that way, so he did his best to keep it in check. He also made a conscious effort to avoid making it obvious to everyone else how he felt.

Besides that, the rest of the wait staff were friendly and seemed to like him, the kitchen staff too. Ivan the chef appeared to take a liking to him and they chatted often after work over staff drinks. He came to realize that Donal was right about his goulash and goose leg, they were special and were unlike anything Andrew had ever eaten before. Donal still made it clear to Andrew that it was his size and stature that kept Ivan from picking on him, something he joked about quite often with both employees.

Donal was also right about Danny Carson. For a 'silent' partner, Andrew felt he sure showed up a lot. He'd shown up at least every Friday to be exact. Also, he'd pop in once or twice during the week to say hello. He arrived usually Friday evenings around nine, ate dinner then hung out in the front bar and hassled Donal for the evening. Andrew still wasn't sure what to make of him. He seemed friendly when he wasn't coming across as arrogant. He talked a lot and about everything, but at the same time always gave the impression he knew more than he actually said. His opinions were many, forceful and varied, but each seemed equally important to voice with clarity, making sure his logic was understood by all. Andrew thought he was borderline offensive at first, but found he was one of those people that grew on you the more time you spent with him. He decided he liked him at the very least. Once he realized half of what he said was for comedic effect, Andrew found he was much easier to get along with than he originally thought. Also, the more he got to know him, the more he began to think the dangerous man he'd heard of through whispers back home existed more in stories than anything else. Still, he wasn't going to rush to find out the truth. He'd grown comfortable being around him and that was enough for now.

Considering his consistent visits, it was no surprise when Danny Carson walked in after nine pm that Friday. He took a seat at the bar that was closest to where Donal stood greeting people at the door. He usually took that seat so he could chat to Donal while he worked, but also it meant he wasn't taking up space for any other customers. 'Taking up a table is like throwing money out of my own pocket.' He had said. Also, the bar area was more casual and conducive to having conversations with many people at once. A table in the dining room would have him confined to speaking to only his waiter.

Andrew watched him walk in through the door and head into the bar. He started over towards him to say hello. He made a point of going over and saying hi every time he was in provided it didn't disrupt his work very much. He owed him for getting him the job, so it was part of how he said thanks. He watched him pull off his light jacket and wrap it around the back of one of the tall chairs in the bar. He saw him say hi to Donal and watched him point to the Guinness tap and hold up his index finger to order a pint. Andrew slid into the bar area and walked up to Danny's table. 'Hey Danny. How's it going?'

'Andrew. Going good. Glad it's Friday, I had a busy week.' Danny said as he let the buttons out of his shirt cuffs and flipped up his sleeves to his forearms. 'How about you? Donal tells me you're working hard and you've picked up a lot quickly. Glad you didn't drag my good name through the mud.'

Andrew nodded. 'Yeah, I think I'm doing okay. Everyone here's been great. They've taken time to show me anything I've asked, so yeah, I'm feeling good about it. I'm picking it up at least.'

'Good.' He said. Andrew followed Danny's eyes as he looked around the restaurant. He pushed out his bottom lip and looked back at Andrew after scanning the dining room. 'Looks like a pretty slow night. Too bad.'

'It's slow now I guess, but it's nearly nine thirty. We had a good crowd in earlier on, but not much of a late crowd.' Andrew said.

Donal walked in from the kitchen and joined them at the

bar table. 'Distracting my waiters I see Carson.' He said.

'Not busy enough to matter Donal. Where the hell is the Friday rush? The place looks dead.'

Donal looked around the dining room then back at the two men. He nodded and said, 'You're right. Is there a match on I'm not aware of or something? It's too slow for a Friday.'

'Don't think so' Danny said. Andrew just shrugged, he hadn't gotten into the Irish sports in the month he'd been there, so he wouldn't know if there was an important game on anyway.

'We can't take too many Friday nights like this anyway.' Donal said. 'Pretty soon, we'd all be in the bread line.' He looked at Danny, 'You get a drink?'

Danny nodded and pointed at the bartender who had the Guinness in his hand walking it over. He put it gently onto the table. 'Thanks' Danny said. The bartender brought over a menu too and Danny opened it up and flipped to the middle looking for the insert that Ivan put in there for the specials. With his head down he asked, 'Ivan making goulash?'

'No, it's not on there tonight.' Andrew said.

'Damn it.' Danny said. 'Really wish he kept it on the standard menu.'

'It's summer Danny' Donal said. 'Who the hell eats spicy

soup in the summertime?'

Danny held up his hands, 'Not for lack of effort.' He said.

'What's he got on there?'

'It's a seafood risotto' Andrew answered for Donal and before Danny could find the insert.

'Look at you showing your skills.' Danny said. 'Okay Andrew. Sell it to me, what's it like.'

Andrew looked at Donal. Donal shrugged and said 'Let's hear it.'

'Okay. It's delicious. It's made in a butter base and with Chicken Stock. Ivan adds chopped parmesan cheese and mixes it in to give it a fuller texture. He mixes in chopped courgettes, prawns and chunks of salmon that he lightly fries first in olive oil and garlic. He serves it with a small triangle toast. It's very rich, but very nice.' Andrew said, then waited for a response.

Donal gave him an approving nod. 'Not bad Andrew' Danny said. 'Okay, you sold it to me, give me that.'

'What about wine?' Andrew asked. 'It goes well with pinot grigio.'

Danny laughed. 'What are you running sales training drills here Donal?' he said.

'No, but the kid does spend a lot of time with Ivan.' Donal answered.

'I guess I do' Andrew said. 'But Ivan's pretty explicit with us about highlighting what he wants us to focus on in our specials' description.'

'I guess so. Anyway, it sounds good, put it through for me. And tell Attila the Hun I'm out here and to come have a drink when the last order's out.' Danny said.

'Will do Danny.' Andrew said and walked out back to drop the slip. Outback the kitchen was slower than usual. The staff were still working and Ivan was finding things to yell about, but Andrew could definitely see that Danny and Donal were right. For a Friday night, it was dead. 'Less tips to share out' he thought, but wasn't too concerned. He decided that, as long as he had enough to live on currently, having a job he enjoyed for a change was the important thing. He wrote the time on the slip and yelled 'Fire it' when he dropped it down for the kitchen staff. 'It's for Danny' he said 'Ivan he's looking for you for a drink when you're finished up back here.'

Ivan looked over and yelled back 'Tell him, he buys, I drink.'

'I will' Andrew said. He headed back out to the dining room and did a loop around his tables, seeing if anyone needed anything, which they didn't. Most tables were finishing their main courses or already done and having dessert and coffee. He walked past a couple of Vicky's tables and noticed the people had finished. He asked if they needed anything and both indicated they were ready for the bill. He continued moving around and started doing some cleaning around the wait station. He was looking around the dining room for Vicky when one of the other waiters walked by and Andrew asked 'Hey Conor, you seen Vicky?'

'Saw her a while ago, pretty sure she walked outside' he said and continued walking past. Andrew realized it had been a while since he'd last seen her, which was curious since she was always good with staying close to her tables. He walked over towards the front door and looked outside, but he couldn't see her. He walked around to the front window and peered out, trying not to lean over any of the tables that sat tight to the glass.

He couldn't see her at first, but spotted her eventually. She was a few yards away from the restaurant. She was talking to a man who looked about Andrew's age. Andrew looked closely and could see they were arguing. He saw Vicky was crying. That was twice he'd seen her cry in a month. He watched for a minute, not sure whether he should worry about her. Then he felt for a moment that he was invading her privacy and decided to turn away. Just before he did, he saw the man shove her and she fell back onto the ground.

Andrew's mind went blank. Before realizing he'd

moved, he was out the front door and walking quickly down the street towards her. He saw she had gotten up and was walking towards him. The man who shoved her started after her again. She picked up her pace and ran past Andrew. The man started jogging and calling after her. Andrew put his hand to the man's chest to stop him as he tried to shove past. 'Get your fucking hand off me!' he said to Andrew. Andrew gripped the man's shirt and stiffened his arm. The man tried to twist Andrew's arm loose forcefully. Andrew shoved him backwards. 'Take a walk.' Andrew said and pointed down the street. 'Fuck you, this has nothing to do with you.' The man said.

'I watched you shove Vicky, so now it does.' Andrew replied.

'Who the fuck do you think you are?' the man said and tried to push past Andrew again. Andrew shoved him back with two hands this time. 'I'm her friend and I said take a fucking walk.' Andrew felt the air deaden around him. Pedestrians rushed quickly around them to avoid walking through any conflict.

'Ya bud.' The man said 'Before what? You think you make me fucking nervous?'

Andrew saw the man tense up at the shoulders and shift his feet to steady his balance.

Andrew tried to keep his breathing steady and his limbs

loose and relaxed, he said. 'I don't give a shit what I make you. But you're not going after her again.'

'Fine' the man said and turned like he was going to begin walking away. Andrew didn't buy it. He could see the man's blood was up and that he wasn't backing down so easily. The man pivoted on his left foot and came around with this right fist swinging for Andrew's face. Andrew saw the pivot of his foot and the man's weight shift like it was delivered in slow motion. By the time his fist came close to where Andrew's face had been, Andrew had already bounced back half a foot and watched the punch sail by in front of him hitting nothing but air. The man put everything he had into the swing and fell forward with the momentum. Andrew snatched out quickly with his left hand and grabbed the man's shirt in the middle of his back. He kicked out hard with the side of his left foot into the back of the man's knee, bringing him down on the same knee. With his free hand, Andrew grabbed the back of the man's belt and gripped it tightly. He spun the man around and using his weight and the spin's momentum, stepped forward and rolled the man onto the cement.

The man hit the ground hard and rolled a few feet forward on the cement. He got up as quickly as possible. Andrew could see he was in pain both from the fall and from his damaged ego. He looked up at Andrew. Andrew shook his head slowly, urging the man to reconsider. He didn't. He dropped his head and ran hard at Andrew. He attempted to tackle him, but Andrew stepped aside and tripped the man. He fell back onto the ground, but jumped up quickly and started swinging wildly. He hit Andrew a couple times with punches, but nothing landed square. Andrew covered up and most either landed on his arms or missed him completely. As he covered his head Andrew read the timing of the swings and began to time his ducks to move away from the punches. Within seconds, the swings started coming in slower. Andrew used the opportunity to push the man back and create space between them. The man paused for a moment then rushed him again. This time Andrew didn't bother jumping out of the way. He timed the rush and lashed out with a quick left jab, then right cross. On the tail end of the right cross, he dipped low, then pivoted and came up with a left hook to the man's cheek. The man was stung by the first two blows and too slow to avoid the last. His knees buckled and he hit the ground within seconds. Andrew stopped himself from coming across with a boot at the last second. The man was moving on the ground but it was slowly and Andrew saw he was done. A strong arm came across his chest from behind and grabbed him. Andrew was caught off guard and tensed in response. 'It's Danny.' Danny Carson said in his ear as he pulled Andrew towards him back through the door of the restaurant. 'That dude's done, get your ass in inside before the guards pick you up.'

Minutes later, the Guards did show up. But by the time they did, the man had left. He took a number of statements from people leaving the restaurant who had seen what happened through the window. He also spoke with Donal and Danny, then with Vicky and finally with Andrew himself.

They seemed convinced Andrew had acted in self-defense and left within an hour. By that time, the slow night at the restaurant had grown even slower and Donal decided to flip the closed sign on the door twenty minutes early. The other staff were abuzz with the excitement from the evening's events, but Andrew was sullen. He noticed Vicky was too. Donal must have understood the body language because he decided that he'd buy the staff drink in the bar next door instead of in the restaurant. He gave Vicky the key and asked her to lock up. Andrew stayed behind with Vicky to finish cleaning up and also so she wouldn't be by herself.

When the others left, Andrew and Vicky continued cleaning for a few minutes. Andrew felt awkward and wasn't sure what to say. Finally, he said. 'I'm sorry Vicky.'

Vicky looked at him with scrunched eyebrows in reply.

'What do you have to be sorry for?'

He shrugged, 'I mean . . . I guess I'm sorry if I put my nose somewhere it shouldn't have been. You know, if I got into your business.'

'Don't be ridiculous.' She said 'I'm the one who's sorry. You could've gotten hurt. He went after you because you were sticking up for me.'

'I guess so.' Andrew said. 'Still.' He shrugged his shoulders again.

Vicky stopped cleaning and walked closer to where he stood. She paused for a moment looking at Andrew, 'It's not what you think though Andrew.' She said.

'I'm not sure what you mean.'

'I guess, I mean, I'm not one of those girls who goes after bad boys or something. I only went on a few dates with that guy, then broke it off cause he's an asshole. He's crazy or something, I guess that's why he couldn't take it. Now every time I see him he makes a scene.'

Andrew pulled up a chair at one of the bar tables and took a seat. The cleaning was done to begin with as they both were thinking about how to start the conversation. Vicky walked into the bar and reached behind it and underneath into the refrigerator. She pulled out two bottles of beer and opened them. Then she came over to the table and handed one to Andrew. He took it and said, 'thanks.'

Vicky walked around the table and took the seat across from him.

'You know, I saw you the first morning I arrived in Dublin.' He said. He took a sip from the beer. She took one from her own beer too.

'I know you did.' She said. 'I remembered you.'

'You did?' he asked.

'Of course I did. I just wasn't sure if you remembered me, so I didn't want to say it to you.'

Andrew laughed. 'Me too. Same reason I didn't say it to you.'

Vicky smiled and laughed as well. Andrew thought often about her smile. She had dimples that only showed up when she smiled. Andrew loved to see her smile and laugh because it made her even more beautiful whenever she did. He found himself staring and dropped his eyes to his hands, both of which held the beer bottle on the table. 'So that night, or morning I guess. Was that why you were crying.' He asked.

'Was I crying that night?' She said as if to herself. 'Yes, I guess I was. I ran into him and he wouldn't leave me alone all night, so I left the nightclub where I was with some friends, but he kept following me.'

'This guy sounds dangerous.' Andrew said.

'Yeah, I guess he was.' She said and slid her chair back

an inch and stood up, stepping closer to where Andrew was sitting.

'What do you mean he was Vicky? He probably still is.'

'I doubt it now.' She said.

'Why's that? What's changed?'

'Well . . . now I have you to protect me . . . Don't I?'

She looked at Andrew and appeared to be trying to keep a straight face. He leaned back slightly at first, but then relaxed in his seat again and smiled. 'Yeah, okay Vicky. I'll protect you.' He said.

'Good.' She said and slid closer to Andrew. Andrew turned in his chair towards her. His hands dropped too, away from the beer bottle he'd been holding. She edged closer to him again, so that she was inches from his face.

Andrew looked in her eyes first, then dropped his gaze down to her lips. He could smell her perfume and her shampoo. Her dark hair glistened under the dim restaurant lighting. He could feel her body heat and could hear his heart beating loudly as it thumped faster in his chest. Then he smiled slightly again at her, looking back into her eyes. 'Good.' He said and leaned in and kissed her.

CHAPTER TWENTY-TWO

Andrew was restless that night in bed. Though he'd fallen asleep in near bliss, at some point during the night he slipped into a nightmare. His dream had him transported back to America. He saw himself standing in the woods along the edge of a golf course he knew well as a teenager in Quincy. He stood in a clearing. It was covered with pine needles that cut his shoeless feet. The surrounding trees were bare and the air wintry cold though he stood in a t shirt and jeans only. Fear gripped him in the dream. Along the edge of the clearing he could see the bodies. They were the four missing girls from Quincy all found dead. He recognized Gina, she lay lifeless at the foot of a barkless tree with eyelids open though her pupils were fogged over. Then everything grew blurry. His brother Brian appeared, though it only looked vaguely like Brian, his hazy memory distorting his features so that he was paler and elongated like a walking El Greco painting. The distorted Brian only said one thing, but said it over and over. It was a question. 'Couldn't you have done something?' he asked, continuously stressing the word *something*. In his dream, Andrew could hear things, but was mute so could not reply. Brian slowly faded into invisibility. Next the man who had gone after Vicky appeared and came after Andrew. Andrew was running but every glance back saw the man gaining on him. His final glance behind him showed that the man after him was no longer that from outside the restaurant, but the three men who attacked him in prison. Andrew tried to pick up speed, but his legs dragged in his dream as if running in a shallow pool. He stumbled through a block of trees and spilled into another clearing. Inside the clearing, the trees thickened around him. He looked around frantically for a way out. He walked into the center then heard the brush shift behind him. He turned and saw Vicky. She was kneeling down and her eyes were red from crying. Next to her was a younger John Bishop. He stood looking at Andrew and laughing. He grabbed Vicky's hair and held up in his other hand a large knife.

That was all Andrew remembered when he awoke with a start, which was plenty. It was morning already and he went over to the window and lifted the shade. Outside was dull and it looked like a light rain fell overnight as the ground looked to be damp, though not newly soaked. He walked into the kitchenette and poured himself a large glass of orange juice. He flicked the television on in the living room for some background noise. He pondered whether to eat breakfast or do some exercise first. It was one of his few days off, in fact there were a rare two days in a row that he had to himself. He decided a jog might do his mind some good. Going for a run helped him focus his thoughts, as long as he left the Ipod at home. He wanted to forget his dream and wanted to clear his head so he could accurately assess what the night before meant. He really liked Vicky and got the impression she felt the same for him. They had kissed. That was all they'd done, but it was long and to him felt like it meant something. 'But, there's so much she needs to know first.' He thought. 'And if I tell her everything . . . she might run.'

He put on his gym shorts and a rugby tech shirt with a t shirt over it. He tied his sneakers while he watched a Top Gear repeat in the background. He took a few minutes to stretch out then headed outside. He turned west toward Rathmines village and started jogging. By the time he reached the small shopping center just minutes away, he already felt better. His blood was flowing and his muscles warm. Both helped to clear his mind, melting his concerns into the background at least while his legs and arms pumped. He continued running and eventually looped around several other South City Dublin villages, each a near mirror image of the other. Each had their own small restaurants, various pubs, butchers and a bookmakers. He finished the loop and ended up back at the Triangle in Ranelagh. It was a few miles at least and he ran it at a good rate so that he was sweating heavily by the time he reached the Triangle. He stopped there and stood for a minute with his fingers locked on top of his head. He continued to pace back and forth as he got his breathing back under control and his body began to cool down. He took his time walking slowly back to his apartment. With nothing much on his agenda for the day, there was no reason to rush.

Back at the apartment, he stood for a long while under the electric shower and let the hot water pour over him. The steam build up created a sauna in the bathroom. He got out and slowly got dressed. Physically, the jog did him well and he felt refreshed and energetic. Mentally, the workout shook off the morning cob webs and he was able to think more clearly.

He poured a bowl of cereal and took a seat on the couch. Halfway through his bowl his doorbell rang. He walked over to the front window, pulled the curtain aside and looked outside. He could see the street below, but couldn't make out who had rang the doorbell. The apartment building had an intercom system recently installed. Andrew walked to the buzzer and held the talk button. 'Who is it?' he said then held down the second button to listen. 'Hey bodyguard' the voice said 'let us in. It's Danny, I'm here with Vicky.'

Andrew paused for a moment. 'That's odd, why are they here?' he thought. He pushed in the talk button again. 'I'll buzz you in' he said, 'I'm the top floor.' then let held down the buzzer He waited by the door, but wasn't comfortable leaving the door ajar until he heard Danny's voice close up. A minute later there was a knock on the door. 'What gives Dawson?' Danny's voice said from outside. Andrew turned the locked and opened up the door. He opened it a crack at first and peeked out. He saw Danny standing there with a confused look on his face. Vicky was behind him smiling. He opened the door fully, 'come on in.' he said.

'Jesus, Dawson, you nervous prick. Who are you expecting?' Danny said as he walked in and took off his jacket. 'I wasn't expecting anyone. Can't say I get many people dropping by.'

'I get it kid. Not everyone's a fan of the pop in.'

'It's not that' Andrew said. 'Anyway, come on in. Make yourself at home.' Danny continued into the living room and walked into the kitchenette. Vicky lingered behind him. She smiled at Andrew when he locked the door and turned back towards them.

'Sorry, it's a small place.' He said.

'I think it's nice.' Vicky said. 'You could do much worse

than this.'

Andrew laughed, 'yeah I know, I've seen worse.'

'I believe it. Even the nice parts of Dublin aren't without some slumlords.'

'Here' he said and walked over and cleared a sweatshirt and loose blanket off the couch. 'sit down, make yourself comfortable.'

'Thanks Andrew' she said and dropped into the couch.

'Can I get you a coffee or tea or something?' he asked.

'Coffee!' Danny yelled from the kitchenette. 'I see you've got a French press. I'd love a coffee.' He walked over to a small table with two chairs in between the living room and kitchenette and sat in one of the chairs.

'Okay' Andrew said. He walked over to the sink and filled the kettle. He flicked the switch on for the kettle. He pulled the coffee out of the cabinet and scooped it into the French press.

'It is a decent place Dawson. No parking though. I left the car in the supermarket in the village.'

'Sorry Danny. I don't drive here anyway.' He said as he poured out the water into the French press. He brought it over to the table with a few cups and some milk.

'So what can I do for you guys? I'm guessing there's a reason you dropped over.'

Danny poured two cups and walked one over to Vicky

on the couch. 'Well Dawson.' He said. 'How long you been living here now?'

Andrew took a sip from his cup before answering while he tried to count the weeks in his head. 'It's over a month now anyway.' He said. 'Went by fast.'

'Yeah I bet.' Danny answered. 'So, you've been here a month already and you haven't even gone to see your mother yet.'

Andrew looked over at Danny, then at Vicky. The comment took him by surprise. Then again, the entire visit did too. 'Did I tell you my mother lived here?' he asked, leaving the question open to both of them. He couldn't remember ever talking about her, but decided he might have said it at some stage and not recalled.

Vicky shrugged and shook her head. Andrew looked at Danny who did the same. 'Not that I remember. But, you gotta know this. We live in a small world sure, but in that world, you're living in a really small country.' Danny said.

'Okay, but what does that mean, really?' Andrew asked.

'It means we have mutual friends Andrew.'

'Really?'

'Yeah, really. My wife's in Donegal. Same town as your mother.'

'Oh' Andrew said.

'What?'

'It's just that . . . I didn't realize you were even married.'

'Well, you never asked.' Danny said. 'I am. But, I work in Dublin, my wife Michelle lives in Donegal. It's complicated, but yeah, I'm married.'

'So it wasn't really a coincidence then.'

'What's that? Me and you meeting?'

'Yeah, did you know who I was then?'

'Ah, come on kid, I had an idea.' Danny said. He let his eye contact with Andrew linger for a few seconds. 'I'd heard of you at least. Plus, you look just like him.' he said.

Andrew gave him a funny look. 'You . . . knew my brother?'

Danny shrugged 'I knew him Andrew yeah . . . But that was many years ago.'

Andrew nodded. He wanted to know more, but he wasn't sure now was the time. He looked over at Vicky and asked 'What about you Vicky? You have family in Donegal too?'

'Me? God no. I've never even been there, I'm from Dublin. I just thought it would be fun to tag along . . . if you'll have me?'

He considered the question for a moment before replying. 'I don't see why not. So, what? We're heading to Donegal? The three of us?' Andrew asked.

'Why not Dawson? I'm going that way anyway. I'll take

you. You have a few days off right? That's what Vicky said. I'll go see my wife. You can let your mother know you're alive. Seems like a no brainer.'

Andrew looked at Danny, then back at Vicky again. He considered the offer for a minute, but knew he had to go. 'Okay' he said. 'Yeah, what the hell, I'll put some clothes in a bag and we'll go.'

'Good' Danny said and stood up. 'Thanks for the coffee.' He walked over to the front door and opened it. 'I'll get the car and meet you both out front in five minutes.'

CHAPTER TWENTY-THREE

It had been several years since Andrew had stepped foot in Donegal. He was still really a child the last time he was there. The route that Danny drove there seemed different from that he remembered. Back then he remembered passing through many more towns and driving for longer on smaller roads. The road network had expanded through some of the Celtic tiger years it appeared, although the motorways never seemed to last as long as they should and the journey northwest still took them through several towns and more than a few periods of one lane roads where one slow driver could result in a traffic backup that stretched for miles. Andrew took the front passenger seat. He wasn't used to being in a situation where he needed to pass other drivers out by pulling into the oncoming lane. Every time Danny did so, Andrew felt his heart rate increase, though by the time they hit Sligo, he'd grown accustomed to it and no longer had to clamp his eyes shut until they were safely back in the correct lane.

After passing Sligo's city center, the surroundings grew familiar to Andrew. He remembered the stretch of beach that ran along the west of the county line, the sandy shoreline was a landscape made for postcards. Also, he remembered the name of the mountain when he saw it, Benbulben. The odd shaped mountain was carved by glaciers during the ice age. It was an impressive spectacle even as a child, but what he remembered more clearly was laughing with his brother at the sound of its funny name.

They drove on through Sligo, passing through Leitrim and onto a newly constructed bypass into Donegal. Danny turned off a short distance later and took them through the town of Ballyshannon. Andrew thought it looked similar to how he remembered it. It was still quaint, though there were more bookmaker shop fronts than he remembered. Also, the center of the town now held a statue of the Irish blues and rock legend Rory Gallagher, who was born in the town. They continued through the town and out past the road leading towards Rossnowlagh beach. Danny slowed to a stop a few miles away from the beach entrance in front of a small cottage. The house looked old and badly in need of painting. Also, the front grass was not well kept and several shrubs were overgrown and blocked much of the walkway leading to the front door. The view from the house however was beautiful. Andrew stepped out of the car and walked to the front, he turned with his back facing the house and could see Rossnowlagh and the ocean in the distance. Green cliffs dropped steep into a long sandy beach that stretched out for over a mile in the distance, eventually wrapping around grasslands and small sand dunes. He could see a few cars moving slowly on the sand itself and when he looked more closely could spot surfers in the water around the beach. He breathed in the sea air that blew across the land from the Atlantic Ocean. He held it in his lungs for a ten count before releasing his breath. 'Well?' he said to Danny, as Danny opened the driver's door and climbed out. 'Well nothing.' He pointed up to the front door. 'This is your Mom's place.' She's expecting you.

Andrew looked over at Vicky as she also stepped out from the car and stretched her arms over her head. She had fallen asleep in the back for the last part of the journey. Before she was in ear shot, he asked Danny quietly, 'Are you both coming in too?'

Danny shook his head slowly. 'I'm not, but she is.'

'Okay' Andrew said. 'You sure you won't come in, even for a second?'

'Sorry, got my own agenda buddy. I got you here, but that's as much as I can do. I'll give you a call tomorrow morning and see how you're fixed.' Danny said.

'Alright' Andrew said. 'Thanks for bringing me Danny.'

'Forget about it, it was my pleasure.' He held out his hand and Andrew shook it. He walked back over to the car and grabbed his and Vicky's overnight bags from the back. Vicky walked around the car and joined him at the walkway. Danny turned the ignition and waved one last time before he slowly pulled away. Andrew turned towards Vicky. He felt awkward and put his head down. 'So . . . just us then.'

She smiled 'looks that way, yeah. Will we knock now or are you still procrastinating?'

Andrew looked up at her. He smiled back and said 'you're right, I'm stalling. Come on let's go.' They continued down the walkway leading to the front door. There was a small step up to a platform. Andrew stepped onto it and knocked heavily on the door. He turned back towards Vicky and smiled again and shrugged his shoulders. He heard steps making their way to the door on the other side of it. He heard a lock click and the door opened. His mother pulled the door open and stepped back in to let him enter. 'Hi Ma' he said and she hugged him, squeezing tightly around his back. 'My baby's finally come to visit. Took you long enough for fuck sake.'

'Sorry Ma, I meant to come up sooner, but it's been busy in Dublin, with my job and getting settled and everything.'

'I know it has' she said 'here come in, come in.' She stepped aside and let him walk further into the hall. Vicky followed, slowly behind.

Andrew grew suddenly aware of the tightness in the hallway while the three of them stood in it. 'Sorry Ma, this is my . . . uh, friend, Vicky. She works with me at this restaurant in Dublin.'

Andrew's mother looked at Vicky then slowly raised her hand. Vicky held it and shook it lightly. 'Nice to meet you Mrs. Dawson.' Vicky said.

'When I heard Andrew was bringing a friend up with him, I didn't expect one so . . . young and beautiful. Please call me Rita.'

'I'm Vicky.'

'Well, come in please. I'll put the kettle on.' Rita said and led them into a small kitchen at the end of the hall. She filled the kettle under the tap and hit the button to start it boiling. She took down three cups from the cupboard along with a clay tea pot.

Andrew dropped his and Vicky's bags outside in the hallway. He circled the small kitchen table and stopped in front of the refrigerator. The face of the fridge was bare for the most part except for a small magnet white board that had nothing written on it. He was surprised to see the refrigerator door so empty. As a young boy, he remembered it overflowed so often with graded tests, pictures drawn during school or photos taken of his brother and himself. It was usually so full that when he shut the refrigerator door, one or two items fell to the floor from the impact. He turned to the table and sat in one of the chairs in the small kitchen. Vicky waited for Andrew to sit down before joining him. 'Is there anything I can help you with?' she asked Rita.

'No thank you Vicky, please make yourself at home.'

Rita finished making the tea and brought the pot and cups to the table and brought out a packet of digestive biscuits and other chocolate bars from a cabinet. She then joined Andrew and Vicky sitting down. They made small talk for a while at the table. Andrew told her all he could think of about the job at the restaurant, including how he came to meet Danny Carson and end up working there in the first place. Rita spoke whimsically, Andrew assumed for Vicky's benefit, about what Andrew was like as a child. 'He was much less reserved.' She had said 'In fact, he was very funny as a child and often the family depended on him for jokes and laughter.'

Andrew didn't like the direction that the conversation was headed or the implication that he no longer had as good a sense of humor. So, he steered the conversation back to his mother. He asked about how she was settling in Donegal and about the health of his Grandmother, who was nearing ninety years old. The obvious topic he stayed clear from was anything to do with his lock up or the unsolved murder of the girls in Quincy. He read into his Mother's body language that she was also purposely staying away from those topics, though he couldn't tell from her manner whether it was for Vicky's benefit or if it was genuinely still too painful or embarrassing to think about.

After a few hours, she made them a small dinner and showed them where they could sleep, awkwardly presenting options that included them staying in the same bed if that was what they were used to. Andrew and Vicky both blushed with embarrassment before Andrew said he'd stay in the sitting room on the couch and Vicky could sleep in the spare bedroom. Rita urged them to take a walk down to the beach while the evening had a stretch of sunlight in the early summer. She insisted they walk by themselves and she would stay behind and clean up after dinner.

They left the house and walked along the edge of the road in the direction of the beach. There was a small laneway that they cut through that halved their journey. They came to a small inn that had a bar and restaurant attached. It was perched at the top of a steep hill that led down a path to the beach. Vicky sat down at a picnic table out front of the restaurant, while Andrew walked inside to see about getting drinks. He ordered two beers from the bar and took them back outside. He sat down next to Vicky on the picnic table and put the drinks down in front of them.

They both faced out towards the sea. The sun was still out, but it was a cool evening and there was a breeze coming off the ocean. 'Some view.' Vicky said and took a sip from her drink. 'It is.' Andrew said. 'I don't think I've ever seen anything like it.' Across from them the wind coming off the ocean made the water ripple and the late evening sun glistened off the waves as they formed. They were closer now to the beach and could see everything more clearly than before in front of the house. A few cars still remained on the sand mostly in front of the hotel that sat at the beach's edge. The vehicle owners were likely made up of either those individuals surfing in wetsuits or those jogging or walking pets along the sand.

'It's a nice break from Dublin definitely. I can't believe you waited a month to come out here. With all this' she swept her hand across the landscape. 'Not even considering your poor Mother.' Vicky said.

'You've never been here at all I thought. So I don't think you can talk.'

'Okay I guess so, but I never had any reason to come here before. Now I have a good one.' She said.

'I'm assuming you mean me and not just the scenery.' He said and smiled.

'Maybe.' She said 'Maybe not.'

He laughed at her. 'Good. So, you're glad you came

along then.' Andrew asked.

'Of course I am. It's beautiful out here. Plus, it was nice to meet your Mother, she seems really nice. Really, she's not like any other Irish mother I've met. She's very . . . accepting of me. Not sure that's typical of mother's meeting girls that their sons bring home.' She said and smiled.

'Really?' Andrew asked. 'Could be the years in America, but I don't ever remember her being any different.'

'I mean it as a good thing.' Vicky said. 'Also, I feel like I know you a little better now.'

'Really? Is that a good thing?' he asked.

'I think so.' She answered. 'I was glad to learn you weren't always just this big guy that walked around all quiet and nervous all the time.'

'Is that how I come across? Quiet and nervous?' Andrew asked.

'Don't forget the big part.' Vicky said.

Andrew smiled. 'Right, and big of course.'

'Truthfully though Andrew, you are so quiet and you do seem nervous often . . . or something like it I guess. I just feel like you're always holding something back.'

Andrew didn't say anything. He took a sip of his drink and looked away for a moment over towards the ocean.

'Sorry Andrew' Vicky said. 'I didn't mean to offend you or anything. I think what I meant is that . . . well, I like you when you're outgoing. You're funnier than I expected and nicer. I think you shouldn't hold back as much. You know. Like the other night. I'm pretty sure that arsehole who you chased off didn't find you quiet or nervous.'

Andrew laughed. 'No, I reckon he did not.' he said. 'Listen, I'm not offended or anything. It's just . . . there's, um, reasons I am the way I am these days. I don't think I was always like that. I guess I'm glad to hear you like me at all.'

She laughed at him and pushed his chest back lightly. 'Of course I do, you eejit. Why else would I be here in fucking Donegal with you? And meeting your Mother no less?'

Andrew brushed her hand away and smiled. 'What about Danny then? To be honest, I'm confused by your whole relationship with him. I thought for a while you too were together. But now, I'm guessing you're not . . . right?'

'Danny? No, of course not. He's a friend alright, but that's all. Danny worked for my father for a pretty long time in Dublin. My father got sick a few years ago and I think I started acting out a bit from the stress of it all. He asked Danny to keep an eye out for me from time to time. I think setting me up with a job that had me working most evenings instead of going out partying was his way of doing that you know . . . and I enjoyed it, so I've been there ever since.'

'Oh, okay, that makes it clearer I guess. I'd been meaning

to ask that for a while.' Andrew said.

'Well now you know. Feel better?'

'I think I do actually.'

'So what about you then Andrew? Are you ever going to tell me your story?' she asked.

Andrew paused. He felt his heart start to race and could feel his face was beginning to blush.

'With the exception of a little bit tonight at your Mother's dinner table, I don't think I've ever heard you talk about anything remotely personal from your past. It's like you were born the day you landed in Dublin. Either that or you have amnesia or something.'

'Sometimes I wish I could forget' he thought, then he said 'There's things . . . reasons I guess, for why I left. I just don't talk about them . . . because I don't know how anyone would react to hearing them.'

'Andrew' she said.

'Yeah?'

'I know about you.'

Andrew leaned back and looked at her, confused. 'What do you mean? What do you know?'

'Well, I know some things. I know you were thrown in jail for some disgusting crimes that you didn't commit. And I know that you were friends with some of those girls that were killed.'

Andrew's eyebrows raised in surprise. 'What? How? Who told you that?' he asked in a high pitched voice.

'Danny did.' She answered. 'When are you going to realize that Danny may not live there anymore, but he's still connected with what goes on in his hometown. By all accounts, you weren't exactly small news either. I'm surprised there wasn't much coverage over here.'

'Who else knows? Who else has he told?'

'I don't know for certain, but I assume everyone at the restaurant knows. Donal definitely does and I'm guessing Ivan too.'

Andrew was flustered. His mind raced and a dozen personal interactions with his co-workers ran through his head. He'd always judged those interactions on the basis that no one knew anything about him. He was overwhelmed by learning that he'd need to reassess everything that happened in the last month, every last exchange he experienced.

'Andrew' Vicky said. 'Just relax.'

He listened to her, 'she must've read the concern on my face' he thought and tried to slow down his breathing and pull himself together.

'Weren't you . . . I mean, aren't you scared off then?' he asked after a minute of catching his breath.

'Sure, I think everyone was a little nervous at first, but

it's not like you actually did those things Andrew. You were wrongly accused. '

'I know I was.' He said. 'I think I just got so used to being judged by anyone who looked at me. Even though I was innocent, people still see you differently once you're accused of something like that. There's always doubt I guess. It's not something that anyone can erase from their memory and I can't really blame them. I was tarnished for life. So, really, I had no choice but to leave. There's no way I could've stayed there and faced that judgment down every last day of my life.'

'So' Vicky asked 'Really, is that why you hadn't come to see your mother? I mean, was that like, part of the reason?'

Andrew looked at her. In a short period of time, he felt like she could read him so well. He wasn't sure how he felt about that, but he was leaning towards he liked it. 'I was afraid.' He answered.

'Afraid to see your own mother?'

'Afraid to look into my mother's eyes and realize that for a time . . . even a fleeting second, she actually believed that I was who they said I was. That I . . . did those things.'

Vicky nodded at his explanation. 'I guess that makes sense.' She said. 'And? Is that what you saw when you looked at her today?'

He shook his head. 'No Vicky. All I saw today was joy.'

'Good' Vicky said and edged her way closer to Andrew so that she was inches from his face. She reached over and took his hand in hers. 'Listen to me Andrew. You did nothing wrong, you hear me? Stop apologizing for everything, you shouldn't do it and you don't need to. And for fucksake, stop walking around with your head drooped down, buried in your shoulders. You have nothing to be ashamed of. You need to keep that big head of yours held up high to show them that, especially if you want people to believe it.' She leaned over and kissed him gently, then laid her head on his shoulder and looked out across the ocean. She slid her fingers past his and interlocked their hands.

He smiled at her and squeezed her hand tightly. 'You're something else.' He said to her.

'Is that right?'

'Yes, I believe it is. You're like medicine.' He said.

She laughed. 'Lousy analogy, but I'll take it assuming it was meant to be a compliment.'

'It's a compliment.' He assured her. 'A very big one.'

CHAPTER TWENTY-FOUR

The countryside's remote silence and utter darkness could be unsettling to those unaccustomed to such things. Andrew had forgotten just how dark the night was, although during the summer months it didn't last very long as the sun returned only a few hours after the twilight turned to black. The heavy curtains in his mother's living room helped to keep the early morning sunrise at bay, however there was no defense from the cows mooing from the neighboring farm outside the window. The animals woke Andrew from a deep, yet uncomfortable sleep on a sofa that was a foot too short length-wise. He stood up and stretched his arms out, then twisted his back left to right quickly to force it to crack. The clock on the wall behind the television showed it was close to eleven am, which was much later than Andrew expected. He and Vicky took a taxi back to the house around one am after they decided it was safer than venturing down the small dark roads with no sidewalks. They stayed up talking in the kitchen for an hour or so when they returned and finished off a bottle of wine that had been opened earlier. Andrew had dry mouth from the wine and his back ached from the awkward sofa, but besides that he felt good from the decent night's rest. Also, there was that lingering joy he had for the opportunity to spend the evening with Vicky. He had that feeling of excitement that comes at the start of new relationships. The more time he spent with her, the stronger his feelings seemed to grow.

He walked from the living room out into the hallway. He could hear voices from the kitchen and walked in their direction. He entered to find Vicky up and dressed, having coffee with his mother at the table. They both looked up to him when he walked in. 'Morning.' He said.

'Morning' they said in unison. Andrew walked over to the counter and found a coffee cup on it and poured himself a cup from the French press and stirred in some milk. He took a sip and turned around to Vicky and his Mother.

'Wasn't sure if you'd ever get up.' Rita said. 'I didn't think you were back that late.'

Andrew reached into the cabinet and pulled down a cereal bowl. 'No, it wasn't that late.' He said. 'I was just tired I guess, been working a lot. Plus I think that's how my body functions now with the restaurant hours. I'm finally adjusting.'

'You sleep alright on that couch?' she asked.

'It was okay Ma. I've stayed on worse.' He said.

'Danny's been by this morning already.' Vicky said. 'He said he'll grab us at one or so to head back.'

'Okay', he said 'thanks'. He took a seat at the table and poured himself some cereal. He looked over to his Mother and said 'Sorry it's such a short trip Ma. Maybe next time I can get a few more days off and stay awhile.'

'Maybe, or I can come see you in Dublin. We were just talking about that.' She said and pointed to Vicky.

'It would be fun.' Vicky said. 'Andrew can take you to the restaurant and show you where we work.'

'Yeah sure, I can do that.' Andrew said with a mouth full of cereal. 'Let me know when Ma.'

They chatted around the table a little longer while they finished breakfast. They made loose plans for Rita's Dublin visit and pegged the timeframe for within the month. Vicky insisted on cleaning up after breakfast and cleared the dishes and started washing them in the sink. Andrew took the opportunity to get dressed and pack up his bag. He showered and shaved then threw on jeans and a t shirt. He folded up the blankets he had in the living room and put them and the spare pillows in his Mother's bedroom. Danny Carson showed up promptly at one o'clock to pick them up. They said goodbye to Rita just outside the door. She gave Andrew a hug. Andrew saw that her eyelids were lined with tears when she let go of him. 'I'm sorry I didn't come sooner Ma. I'll make sure I come up more often.' He said.

She smiled and wiped the slow falling tears from her cheeks. 'I'm glad you're okay Andrew.' She said and hugged him again. 'Me too.' He said softly.

'She's a good one. Worth sticking around for I hope.' she said to him as she waved to Vicky before she got into the back of the car. 'Take care of her Andrew.'

'I know she is.' He said nodding his head. 'I'll try. Bye Ma.'

He turned and walked around to the passenger door and got into the car. Danny waved goodbye out the window, then he did a U-turn in the road to head back towards town. Andrew waved as they drove away, looking back until the house was finally out of view. They drove back the way they came, back through Ballyshannon, then on through Sligo, Roscommon then Longford. Within three hours Danny pulled up in front of Andrew's apartment in Ranelagh. Andrew thanked him and the two men shook hands before he opened the door and climbed out of the car. He stood for a minute with a hand lingering on the car's hood. He looked in the back window at Vicky. He decided he wasn't ready to say goodbye to her just yet. He knocked on the back window lightly with his index finger. She leaned over and pushed the button to bring the window down. When it was half open she stopped and looked out at him. 'Can you stay for a while?' he asked. She smiled at him and put her hand on the bag in seat next to her. 'Of course I can.' She said. She got out of the car and said 'bye Danny' and waved after she shut the door. She joined Andrew on the sidewalk as Danny pulled the car away from the curb. He drove away, tapping the horn once as he did.

CHAPTER TWENTY-FIVE

Andrew peeled apart two slices of bacon and dropped both onto a hot pan. The pork sizzled immediately and a second later spit hot grease at his wrist as he reached over the pan to light the back burner. 'You're up early.' He heard Vicky say from behind him. He turned around to find her standing in the living room wearing nothing but one of his t shirts, which looked like a fat man's poncho draped over her. He smiled at her and said, 'good morning. I thought I'd make you breakfast.'

'Thanks' she said and slid into one of the chairs at the table by the kitchenette. 'What are you making?'

'An omelette' he answered as he whisked two eggs in a bowl with a fork quickly, then poured it onto the round frying pan at the back of the stove top. 'Some bacon too.'

'Sounds great.' She said. 'I didn't know you could cook. Honestly, I wouldn't have pictured it.'

'I'm not sure that I can.' He said. 'I'll let you be the judge. I figured I spend enough time with Ivan listening to him talk about food and watching him work, I'm hoping some of his skills in the kitchen have rubbed off on me.'

'Sure, we'll see.' She said. 'He did take a shine to you.'

'He's a complicated man that Ivan. I listen to him that's all.'

'Is that the trick?' she asked.

'Seems to work for me.' He got a plate down and flipped the omelette in half on the pan, creating a perfect semi-circle. After a couple seconds he transferred it carefully to the plate using a spatula and dropped the bacon next to it. 'Here you go' he said as he put it in front of Vicky with some silverware and a glass of orange juice.

'Thanks Andrew' she said. 'Are you not having anything?'

'No I am. Just don't have a pan big enough to do two at a time. Go ahead and start, there's nothing nice about a cold omelette.' He cracked two more eggs and whisk them quickly, then poured them into the pan to start the process over again. He smiled as he did it. He found that recently he enjoyed trying new things in the kitchen. He never did much cooking before, but in the last month he seemed to do it often. He really liked it and was developing a knack for it. He suspected his interest was mostly drawn from working around good food all the time at the restaurant. His palate was spoiled by the staff meals served before each shift. He was starting to think he may have found his calling. As he prepared his own breakfast, his mind drifted to the night before. He smiled at the images as they played back through his head. Vicky had stayed with him and they made love for the first time. He woke up early and couldn't wipe the smile off of his face. He couldn't sit and wait for her to wake up either, so he decided to start cooking, trusting in the smell of frying bacon to rouse her from her sleep, a method he figured worked for most of the western world.

He made his own plate quickly, without the same finesse or attention to detail he'd shown on Vicky's breakfast. He took the seat across from her. 'Any good?' he asked.

She smiled at him. 'Really good actually. Careful or I might make a habit of this.' She said.

He laughed, 'good, I was hoping that'd be the case.' He started into his omelette when he heard a knock at the door. He looked up at Vicky. She looked back at him and shrugged, 'I don't know' she said. Andrew stood up and took a sip of his juice to wash down the first bite of his breakfast. He slowly walked over to the door. He hesitated before reaching for the lock. It was odd to have anyone stop by really. It was odder that whoever it was didn't ring the doorbell from downstairs first. That meant they were already in the building. He leaned slowly toward the door with his ear, listening for any voices. There was another knock, followed by a man's voice, 'Dawson, come on man, I know you're in there, I can smell your breakfast.'

'Danny? Is that you . . . again?' He looked over at Vicky. She nodded then got up from the table and walked into the bedroom. Andrew opened the lock and opened the door a few inches. Outside Danny Carson stood, with Donal next to him. 'Come on man, let us in. Got something important to talk about.'

Andrew was confused, but opened the door to let them in. Danny walked in first and Donal followed behind him. 'Come on in. Twice in the same week Danny, what's up?' Both men walked into the living room and over to the table. Danny sat down first and Donal sat across from him. He looked down at the table, noticing the two place settings. 'You here with someone?' he asked looking up at Andrew as he walked over and sat on the armchair of the couch. Vicky walked out just then from the bedroom. She managed to throw on jeans and her own shirt. 'Morning Donal. Danny.' Donal smiled and waved back. 'Sorry to intrude' he said and held his hands up.

Danny turned to Andrew, 'Yeah, we're both sorry, but listen Andrew, there's a reason we came by.' He said.

Andrew looked at Danny, he looked more serious than usual. His face had a stern gaze instead of the jocular smirk it usually wore. He looked anxious, which in turn made

Andrew anxious. He slid down from the armchair to the seat of the couch. 'What is it?' he asked looking back and forth from Danny to Donal.

Danny spoke first. 'Bernadette Gleason. You know her?'

'Bernie, yeah of course I know her.' Andrew answered. 'She's my . . . uh, good friend. Why, what's this about?'

Danny crouched down in the chair, leaning towards Andrew. He brought his elbows to his knees and his hands together, resting his chin on top of them. 'There's no easy way to say this Andrew, so I'll just say it. She's missing. There's talk that she's been nabbed by whoever's snatching those Quincy girls.'

Andrew slid further into his couch and pushed his back against the cushion. His mind raced too quickly to isolate any one thought. He brought his hands up to his face and ran them through his hair. 'Oh no Bernie.' He thought. When he didn't say anything for a minute. Danny continued. 'Andrew?'

Andrew looked at him. His eyes were wide open and his jaw slack. 'You understand what I'm saying to you?' Danny asked. 'You know what that means if the same dude does have her?'

The life crawled back into Andrew with a sudden burst of adrenaline. He jumped from his seat. 'I have to go.' He said quickly bouncing on his feet. 'I need to get back there.'

'Andrew' Donal chimed in. 'Think it through for a minute. How much could you even do going back there? I'm not sure there's anything good for you there.'

Andrew looked at Donal, surprised by his interjection. He shook off the tingle of irritation that ran up his spine. 'It doesn't matter Donal. I can't sit here. I need to do something. I don't know what. But, whatever it is I can't do it from here.'

Andrew looked over towards Vicky. He saw a painful look develop in her eyes. He wanted to explain, but he felt there wasn't time, plus he wasn't sure what to say. He reached into his pocket and pulled out his phone. He pressed a button on the side to bring up the time. He turned back to Danny. 'Can you get me to the airport Danny? I have time, but I need to move now.'

Danny stood up and nodded. 'Yeah, Andrew, I'll take you.' Andrew ran into his room and grabbed a backpack and his passport. He stuffed a change of clothes into the bag, then ran into the bathroom and grabbed his toothbrush and deodorant and threw them in also. 'Let's go.' He said.

All four of them went on the journey to the airport. No one said anything during the trip. Andrew sat in the back with Vicky, but he looked out of the window for much of the duration. They pulled up to departures just over twenty minutes later. Andrew reached down and grabbed his backpack. 'Thanks Danny.' He said and pushed the door open. He paused, then reached his hand over and took Vicky's wrist in a light grasp. 'I'm sorry.' He said.

Her eye's looked watery, but no tears had fallen. 'Be safe Andrew.' She said then looked away, out her own window.

Andrew got out of the car and started walking away, but heard the car door open. Danny climbed out and leaned over the top. Andrew looked across at him. 'Are you sure I can't talk you out of this Andrew?' he asked.

'Are you sure you're the right person to try Danny?'

'No matter how it ends Andrew . . . no matter what happens, there'll be . . . regrets. That's if you make it out alright yourself.' Danny said.

Andrew considered his words for a moment. Then he said, 'If you're me right now Danny . . . do you stay?' Danny let out a breath and smiled slightly. 'I hope you make it back here safe Andrew. I've decided I like having you around.' He said and tapped the roof twice.

'Take care Danny.' He said and turned and walked away. He broke into a brisk walk, nearly a run after he cleared the automatic doors and headed straight for the Aer Lingus ticket desk. He made it just in time to purchase a seat on the next flight to Boston.

CHAPTER TWENTY-SIX

When he purchased the plane ticket and made his way through security to the gate, Andrew felt like a six hour plane journey would be sufficient time to align his thoughts and devise some kind of plan of action. When the airplane touched down in East Boston however, Andrew still couldn't figure his next move, never mind having a plan of any description. 'Maybe they were right', he thought. 'What the hell good can I do being here? Who will even talk to me?'

The flight was the longest six hours of Andrew's life. It made his days in prison feel brief and insignificant in comparison. He felt helpless waiting on the plane. He couldn't eat, he couldn't sleep, he didn't want to talk to anyone, and he couldn't listen to music, watch movies or read anything at all. His mind ran circles around itself, most thoughts disappearing in a puff of smoke as soon as they arrived in his head. He just stayed sitting up straight and kept his face buried into the window looking out across the blue sky, then the sea, until eventually he started recognizing neighborhoods from above. Then he began to feel sick, his stomach twisted in knots from a combination of minor turbulence and a familiar unease that he mistakenly thought he had rid himself of in the last month. He thought of Bernie. He could picture her face, in his mind's eye she was smiling. He knew wherever she was now however, she would not be smiling. 'If she's even breathing at all.' He considered, then shuttered at the thought. He couldn't fathom why someone would take her. 'What could they want with her? Why her?' It dawned on him that those close to the other ones, those other girls that were taken, must have felt the same way he did now. He knew the weight of their angst finally and felt guilty for not feeling much of anything before, until it was really someone he loved that was taken. 'Have I become so callous?' he considered.

He didn't check a bag in. He carried his backpack with him on the flight and walked straight from the landing gate through passport control, then downstairs through customs. The customs official looked him up and down sternly. Andrew figured he was likely noting the lack of luggage and deciding whether it was a threat. Finally, he let him through. Andrew used his U.S. passport to travel back, which he assumed quickened the silent interrogation. He walked out into the arrivals hall in Logan Airport's

International terminal. He sifted through the crowds of people waiting for loved ones and spilled out until the sidewalk. He crossed over the street to the taxi stand and was inside a cab within two minutes. The taxi driver didn't say much to Andrew. He was too busy on his cell phone speaking in another language through a blue tooth connector in his ear. Andrew guessed he was Haitian based on the tone of the language that sounded vaguely French. Even stepping into the taxi, he wasn't sure where exactly he was headed and just said 'Quincy.'

As they weaved slowly through traffic down route 93 south Andrew decided he needed access to a vehicle. If he was planning to act with any semblance of speed, he couldn't be depending on taxis and public transport. The driver took a Dorchester exit and swung around towards Quincy. Andrew directed him towards Wollaston Beach, then down the side street to West Elm variety convenience store. Andrew paid the man and climbed out of the taxi.

He stood for a moment on the sidewalk outside the shop, staring in through the window. Nostalgia took him momentarily as he considered the cumulative hours, days, probably weeks of his life he'd spent sitting outside that shop staring into the window. The memories were so many and so mundane, that they seemed to melt into one long waiting period. There were no cars in the lot out front, which he was glad to see. 'Not ready yet to be recognized by random people.' He thought. He gathered himself, then walked up the front steps and reached his hand out to grab the handle. He wasn't sure if Chef would even be working, but he had to try.

The door chimed when he opened it. He stepped inside and felt a blast of cold air from the cooling system that hung just inside the door. He shivered from the unexpected breeze. He looked over at the register, but couldn't see anyone behind it. He walked deeper into the small shop, but there was no sign of anyone. 'Hello?' he said loudly. 'Chef, you around?'

He heard a noise from somewhere and a voice called out. 'Just a minute.' Seconds later, Chef Benson walked out of a small doorway that led to a storage room. He carried a box of potato chips, which he fumbled and nearly dropped when he walked out and saw Andrew. He regained control before placing it down softly at his feet. 'Shit, Andrew. I wasn't expecting to see you.' He said.

Andrew watched him walk around the back of the counter and duck under a door flap. 'Hi Chef.' He said. 'Didn't mean to surprise you. Honestly, I wasn't expecting to be back . . . not so soon anyway.'

'So you've heard?' Chef asked. He leaned against the outside of the counter. He looked tired and more unkempt than Andrew could remember ever seeing him.

Andrew nodded at Chef's question. 'Bernie? Yeah Chef, I heard.'

'I should've guessed you'd be back. You and her were close I know.' Chef crossed his arms nervously in front of his body. 'What are you planning to do?' he asked.

'I'm still thinking on it. But . . . I mean, I have to do something. I think I'll start by talking to that Detective. Does he still come in here?' he asked.

'Harris? Uh, yeah, from time to time he does, sure.' Chef answered. He shifted his hands from across his body and stuffed his fingertips into his jeans' pocket, leaving the thumbs out.

'Do you know how to contact him?' Andrew asked. 'I mean, can you get in touch.'

Chef considered the request for a moment before answering. 'I, uh, I don't have his number. But, listen, I can probably get it. Just might need some time.'

'Okay.' Andrew said. 'How much time to do you need?'

'I don't know, a few hours maybe.'

Andrew paused and put his index finger to his teeth and bit down on the nail. After a few seconds he took it out from his mouth. 'It's gotta be faster than that Chef. This is fucking important. I don't have time to waste man.'

Chef nodded his head in reluctant agreement. 'Yeah,

okay. You're right. Give me an hour though, I need to track down a few people to try and get in touch. Is there a number he can call you on?'

'Shit, not really. Just have my Irish phone. Here' he said and walked over to the counter. He picked up a Keno pencil and took one of the lottery forms and wrote his cell number down. I'll give it to you anyway, but tell him I'm waiting at Mackin's pub for him. I'll wait an hour.' He handed the piece of paper over to Chef, then dropped the pencil back into the holder. He stood standing in front of Chef silently for a minute.

Chef looked at the paper and took in the number. He looked back up at Andrew to see him staring at him. 'Is there something else?' he asked.

'Yeah, one thing.' Andrew said. 'Is my old truck out back? I need to be able to get around.'

Chef dug his left hand into his pocket and fished around for a moment. He pulled out a set of keys and lobbed them underhanded to Andrew. Andrew caught them to his chest, then grasped them in his hand. 'Thanks Chef. You can have it back when I leave.'

'Hey, it's your truck Andrew. I have my car out back there too, so keep the truck as long as you need.'

'Thanks Chef.' He said. He stuffed the keys in his pocket and started to walk over to the door. He looked back as he grabbed the handle. 'Remember. Mackin's. One hour from now.' He said.

'I'll do my best.' Chef said.

'That's all I'm asking.' Andrew said. He paused a moment longer then turned back to Chef. 'Hey Chef.'

'Yeah Andrew?'

'Have you seen Stevie around? I mean recently.'

Chef thought for a moment then said. 'I've seen him since you've been gone, I'm pretty sure. I haven't seen him for a couple weeks though. Aren't you still in touch?'

Andrew shook his head. 'No . . . not currently. If he happens to come by, tell him I'm back.' He said. He turned then and walked out through the chiming door.

CHAPTER TWENTY-SEVEN

Outside of Mackin's pub, Andrew waited for a few minutes in the truck before going in. Sitting in his truck brought back more memories. The smell of the leather seats was still the same. It drove the same and the noises it produced hadn't changed. If there was one thing he did miss from home, it was that truck. It was on its last legs and had been for some time. He could've afforded a new one at any stage, but could never part with it until he was finally forced to. The truck had been his Father's. He had purchased it brand new a year or two before he was killed. To Andrew, it was really one of the only remaining connections to the man. He struggled even to picture his face a lot of the time, but whenever he sat inside the truck and took in its sounds and smells for some reason, he could see his father's face clear as day. He let thirty minutes roll by since he left Chef's store, then decided he'd go into the bar room and wait. He walked inside through the large door and took a seat at one of the tall stools at the corner of the bar. The bartender had to look twice when he saw Andrew. He obviously recognized him, but didn't make a big deal of it. 'What can I get ya?' he asked.

'You have coffee?' Andrew asked.

'I can put some on, sure.' He answered.

'Okay, good, please do.' The bartender walked over to the coffee machine and started fiddling with its dials. Andrew turned around to the clock that hung high up on the wall in the center of the bar room. He noted the time. He wasn't sure what he'd do next if Detective Harris didn't show up, but he wasn't prepared to wait much longer. He knew Bernie was out there, he could feel it. But, every second that ticked by, he sensed she was one step closer to hell. He felt confident that Harris would show up however. Despite their run in, Andrew found himself liking the man. 'Well, at least I respect him.' He thought.

The bartender brought over a coffee. Andrew pulled out his wallet and sifted through it to luckily find a twenty dollar bill stuck in one of the folds. He slid it across the bar. The bartender's fingers snatched it up and he quickly returned with the change. Andrew watched him count out the bills and lay them on the bar, then drop the coins on top of them. When he finished, he walked away to another customer that lined up at the other end of the bar.

A sliding chair grated the floor behind Andrew and he

turned around to find the Detective pulling up a seat next to him. 'Andrew Dawson.' The Detective said and held out his hand.

'Hello Detective.' Andrew said and shook hands with him.

'Didn't think I'd see you again so soon, but considering the circumstances, I'm not surprised.' Detective Harris said.

Andrew nodded. 'So you know why I'm here then?' he asked.

The Detective sat up straight on the tall chair and undid the zipper on his light jacket and shook it out. 'Well, I know the catalyst for why you're here. As to what you're here to do. No, I don't know that.' He answered. 'The question is, do you know?'

'I just can't sit idly by Detective. Bernie . . . she means a lot to me.'

Detective Harris nodded. 'I'm sure she does Andrew. I know a little bit of the history there. Does her fiancé know that?'

Andrew shrugged and held his hands up. 'Don't get the wrong impression Detective. That's not what I'm here about. Bernie's a friend, a good friend. Never mind our history. That's just what it is . . . history.' He said. 'I just want to help. What can you tell me about the case, anything?'

'It's an open investigation Andrew.' He said. 'I think you

know I can't tell you much. I'm not leading the missing person's case, that's another division. But, I am looped in considering . . . . Well you know, considering there's a chance, a very good chance that my cases are related.'

'But do you have leads?' Andrew pleaded. 'Are you out there searching for her?'

Detective Harris looked tired and his tone was sharp. 'Right now, I'm here talking to you Andrew.'

Andrew could see the Detective's patience was worn thin likely from the lack of success in finding the killer, but he wasn't about to be bullied by anyone just now. 'What's that supposed to mean?' Andrew asked.

'Come on. You know the line. Any second I'm talking to you means I'm not out looking for her . . . unless you know something that can help that is. Do you Andrew? Do you know something that could help?' he asked.

Andrew tapped the side of the coffee cup with his fingers. He was growing more impatient each second. His frustration was building at the Detective's unwillingness or inability to share any details. He knew there were protocols the man needed to follow, but was blinded by his anguish. 'No.' he said. 'I don't have any new information.'

The Detective slid his chair back slowly and stood up. He reached into his pocket and pulled out a card. 'Here' he said and slid it across the counter to Andrew. 'I have your number. Now you have mine in case anything does occur to you.'

Andrew lifted the card and stuffed it into his pocket. 'You'll let me know if there's anything I can do to help?' he asked.

'I will.' He answered. He softened his facial expression for a moment and said 'Hey, I know it's tough, but there are good cops on this. We're doing our best to find your friend Andrew.'

Andrew nodded. 'I know Detective.'

'Okay' he said and patted Andrew firmly on the shoulder then he turned towards the door and briskly walked out. Andrew watched him leave. He turned and propped his elbows on the bar and brought he hands up to his head, hugging his ears with his forearms. 'What next?' he said to himself. 'What else?'

He sat that way, with his arms around his head for a couple minutes. He leaned back in his chair and rubbed his eyes. He felt anger start to build within him and could feel his body heat rise with the increased blood flow. 'Fuck this.' He said quietly to himself. He stood up quickly and kicked the chair back behind him. It scraped loudly across the floor and he saw heads turn in his direction. He turned and walked out of the bar quickly and over to his truck. He pulled the door open and jumped in, slamming it shut after him. He fired up the engine and pulled the transmission into drive. He pushed down on the gas so the truck's engine roared as he drove away. He turned a tight left down Newport Avenue, past the back of the Quincy Center train station. He sped down the road, stopping only minutes later at the Beale Street intersection. It was closing in on evening time and the traffic started building. He tapped the steering wheel waiting in a line of cars for the light to change color. Up ahead he could see Dee Dee's lounge. The small bar sat on the corner of Newport Avenue and Brook Street across from Wollaston train station. A line of budget Asian massage parlors lined the pathway to the bar's dilapidated shop front. He remembered a much more vibrant neighborhood in his youth. It had given way to depravity after years of economic downturn.

The light turned green and he hit the gas to move. The cars in front moved slowly off the start line. He felt the pause in the traffic helped him to get his nerves under control. At the next block, he turned down the side street and pulled up to the curb. He killed the engine and pulled the keys out of the ignition. He took in a deep breath, then let it out slowly before pushing the driver's door open and jumping down from the truck. There were very few cars parked on the block. At a glance, it was difficult to tell whether the bar was even open, but he knew it was. Mike

Doyle might be in there. Bishop at least, was in there, he could sense it.

He put his hand softly on the door and pushed it in. It swung in easily and he walked inside. The room was dark. The beer signs behind the bar weren't lit, but a small lamp at the corner of the bar was. Two men were standing near it, one on either side of the bar. Their shadows from the lamp stretched long across the wall behind them. The one on the outside of the bar turned around in his seat, then stood up slowly, peering across at Andrew through the dark room.

Andrew stood still for a moment after walking in, waiting for his eyes to adjust to the drastic change in lighting. Once they did, he continued walking across the room towards the two men. As he approached, he could make out their faces. Neither one was John Bishop. The one that was standing closest to him however he recognized as Mike Doyle. Andrew froze for a moment, though it felt longer to him. He fought to control his breathing, but struggled to do so. He could feel his temples begin to pulse rapidly and his vision blurred and sharpened several times in a matter of seconds, red clouds growing more poignant with each interval. The man took a couple step towards Andrew as he entered the room. Andrew had the lighting in his favor as Doyle walked closer, staring to get a look at his face. 'Help you with something?' Doyle asked.

Andrew took a few more steps, then stopped. He saw in Doyle's face that he recognized him at last. 'I know you . . . Dawson. What fuck do you want?'

'You know what the fuck I want Doyle. Where is she?' he yelled.

Doyle postured his shoulders and brought his hands slowly towards his waist. Andrew's eyes followed his hands, keeping note of any sudden change in the man's stance. 'Get lost Dawson.' Doyle said.

'Fuck you Doyle. Last chance. Tell me where the fuck you have Bernadette!'

Doyle took another step towards Andrew. Andrew slid his right foot back a couple inches. He kept his eyes trained on Doyle's right hand. 'I won't say it again Dawson. Fuck off!' Then he quickly reached under his shirt near his belt.

Andrew didn't wait to see any metal gleam. He wouldn't have caught it in the poor lighting anyway. He brought his right foot up quickly and kicked straight out at Doyle's groin. He connected flush and Doyle fell backwards into the bar. He bounced off the bar, which kept him upright and managed to get a handle on the grip of his revolver. Andrew jumped forward and grabbed his wrist with his left hand and swung a heavy elbow with his right, catching Doyle in the face, but falling over in the process. Blood shot from

Doyle's nose and splattered red across Andrew's face. He wrestled the gun from Doyle's hand on the ground. He heard a loud 'pop' and his hand jerked back as the gun went off in the struggle. The bullet missed both of them, and dug into the wood floor, shooting splinters in the air when it hit.

Andrew freed his right hand and managed to grab the gun away with both hands, burning his palm on the nozzle when he gripped it. He raised both hands and came down hard on Doyle's head with the butt of the weapon. Doyle stopped struggling. Andrew saw a flash of movement from his left just in time to duck out of the way of a whiskey bottle. The man behind the bar had come around the other side and just missed him with the bottle. It broke in pieces off the side of the bar and shards hit Andrew in the face. One long piece of glass broke off and buried itself in the bartender's wrist. He fell back and let out a howl. Andrew jumped to his feet and pointed the revolver at the man. He held it up for a moment to make sure the man wouldn't rush him again, then he spun around back to where Doyle had fallen. He was no longer there. Andrew slowly edged over the bar and scanned behind it to find nothing, he looked around the room but Doyle was nowhere in sight.

He was winded from the fight and had to take a couple breaths before he could get a word out. 'where did he go?' he muttered between breaths 'Where?'

The man sat bleeding before him. He looked to be in pain. He didn't reply with words, but he glanced across the room at a heavy green door hidden in a dark corner. It was enough for Andrew to understand. He backed over towards the door, keeping the gun raised with a shaky hand as he did. When he reached it, he grabbed the knob and twisted. It opened with a creak. He turned and walked into a dark room. He shut the door behind him. A shelf stood beside the door and he tipped it over to obstruct the entrance. He continued into the room and over to another door. The door was ajar and a dim light shone through it. Andrew walked slowly towards it. He kept the gun at his side and pushed the door open slowly with his left hand.

John Bishop sat behind a desk next to a few small television screens. He sat back in his chair and held out his palms when Andrew opened the door fully. Andrew stood in the doorway and looked at the man. He had changed quite a lot since he had last seen him. His hair had gone from black to a stark grey, making him look much older than a man in his thirties. He wore a black fitted military jacket that made it obvious he still took care of himself physically. His face showed weathered lines, especially on either side of his eyes. His skin looked taught and he was tanned, except for a thick white scar that ran under his left eye. It was a reminder of their last encounter. Andrew looked from him over to the television screens. It was CCTV linked to cameras that he must've had in the front bar. Bishop saw him looking at the screens. 'Doyle's gone.' He said calmly.

The adrenaline from the fight with Doyle and the bartender was starting to wear off and Andrew felt weak. He could feel his hands shaking, but for the most part, he seemed to have his emotions back under control. He held the gun in his palm out for Bishop to see. It was slick with blood that also stained Andrew's forearms, wrists and hands. 'Do I need this here?'

'Tell you what Andrew. Hang on to it if it makes you feel safe.' Andrew considered it, then tucked the revolver into the back of his pants.

'You looking for a job?' Bishop asked then pointed to the screens. 'Two positions in my crew just opened up.'

Andrew shook his head. 'We both know that's not why I'm here John.'

'Well then Andrew. Can you enlighten me? Why are you here then? Just to put a beating on my men and shoot off guns in my barroom?'

'The girls John. I need to know what happened to those girls. I need to know where to find Doyle. Where did he run to?'

'Ohh' Bishop said, drawing out the word. 'Your girl goes missing. So now you care is that right? Now you're desperate. So desperate that you come to me.' He smiled and started laughing, the creases in his face growing more pronounced when he did. 'Now you're looking for help?'

'I guess I am.' Andrew said.

'You got a strange fucking way of asking for help.' He said. 'Tell me why I should help you.'

'You owe me John. That's why.' Andrew said.

'I owe you?' Bishop said and pointed at the scar under his eye. 'Remember this?' he asked.

Andrew just nodded.

'I think we could debate about who owes who here.' Bishop said.

'So you won't help me?' Andrew asked.

'No, I would Andrew. Despite that hatred I see in your eyes, I'd definitely help you. Well, I would if I could.' He said. 'But I doubt I can offer anything more to you than you already know.'

'That's bullshit John. This is your city remember. Yours. Not a damn thing goes on in this slime bucket that you don't at least know a little about.'

'Listen Andrew. I don't know shit about any missing girls. I don't know shit about any dead girls either.' He said.

'Come on John.' He pleaded. 'You have to.'

'I have to Andrew? I fucking have to?' he puffed out a breath then he leaned forward onto the desk and stood up.

He was as tall as Andrew and their eyes were level. He stared for a minute at Andrew. Andrew didn't understand his expression, but continued to hold his eye contact.

Bishop let out a breath, then finally spoke 'You still working out a lot to keep that temper of yours under control?' he asked.

Andrew tilted his head slightly and continued looking at Bishop. He waited for more. He didn't know what he was getting at. 'There's a mirror in the bathroom Andrew' Bishop continued, 'I suggest you go take a good long look in it.'

Andrew shook his head. He could feel his blood rising to his head once again, but fought hard to keep his anger down. 'What the fuck does that mean?' he asked through gritted teeth.

'It means you should start looking a little closer to home, if you really want to know who did those things and who has your girl.'

'You implying I did this?' Andrew asked.

'No, you fucking asshole. I'm implying you're either dumb, blind or in denial. Jesus Christ Andrew, the cops had a knife they believed was the one that gutted Gina O'Neil like a fucking fish. They pulled it from your truck, it had your fingerprints and both yours and her DNA. How the fuck could that happen huh? Who could do all that if it wasn't you? I'd say the pool of candidates is pretty fucking small or your tolerance for coincidence is pretty fucking big.'

'I fucking know what the cops had John. It's Doyle's knife. Now tell me where I can find him!'

'Way I see it bud, there's only one piece of information the cops didn't have and that's cause you never offered it.'

'What Johnny, enough with your cryptic bullshit! Fucking get to the point.'

'Where did *you* get the knife Andrew?'

'From Doyle! You know this.' Andrew said.

'You're not hearing me kid. Listen to me, there's a reason Doyle was never brought in. He was in fucking northern New Hampshire with me buying a fucking ski lodge the night Gina O'Neil was killed. So think! Not who owned the knife. I'm asking where did you get it? Who put that knife in your hands? I think I know. But, I *know* that you know.'

Andrew stood up straight. He was stunned to hear what Bishop had to say. He felt weak. He was light headed and his knees began to wobble. He felt his stomach turning and could taste bile rising in his throat. It was obvious. It was obvious to Bishop. Bishop knew Andrew well. He knew there was only one person Andrew worked out with. It was obvious to him now too. When the words left Bishop's mouth, Andrew knew it was true. That niggling thought always in the very depths of his mind, every ounce of logic and intuition stifled by utter denial that penetrated deep into his mind, body and soul. He had always known it. If it wasn't the only possible explanation, it was at least the most likely. 'How else could they ever had mistaken me as the killer?' He knew who had Bernie. It was clearer than any thought he'd had in a lifetime. There was no doubt. He knew it to be gospel. And, he knew where she was too.

He regained control of his legs by putting a hand on the desk that separated him and Bishop to support his weight. He looked up at Bishop, who stood silently witnessing Andrew's dawning realization. He walked around his desk and over to the side of the room. He pushed aside a curtain to show another door. It was a back exit. 'Here' he said. 'Go this way Andrew. I don't think you have much time to waste.' He held the curtain back with one hand and twisted the knob with the other, opening up the door that led to a back alleyway. Andrew said nothing else to Bishop. He slowly stepped over towards the exit and ducked under the curtain. He looked at Bishop one last time in the doorway before turning his head away and heading out into the darkness.

CHAPTER TWENTY-EIGHT

The sun had just about disappeared when Andrew stumbled out of the back alleyway from Dee Dee's lounge and walked quickly, yet unsteadily around the corner back to his truck. He reached Marina Bay in only minutes. There were lights around the marina and the front parking lot was lit up brightly with street lamps and bustling with cars. He drove around the large lot and passed through to a much quieter and darker lot that led up to the dirt pathway. He entered the brush on foot. After a few steps the light from the parking lot was suffocated by the shrubs that hid much of the entrance. He walked down the path, but stayed close to the edge to maintain cover. The air was warm and he began to sweat. There was a breeze off the water that he felt every couple of steps. The cool air against his clammy skin made him shiver. The ground beneath him was soft mud that clamped around his shoes in many spots. He could hear his own footsteps in those moments as it popped when he pulled his feet out to step forward. The pathway was a mile long to the small beach at the end. He tried to keep a quick pace, but was slowed by the need for stealth. He knew the spot's isolation meant that any unaccustomed sound could signal his approach.

It felt like an eternity had passed by the time he could see the entrance to the beach. He ducked behind a row of rough bushes a short distance away and peered out to where the mud turned into sand. He could just about make out the wrinkle of waves in the distance, though the sea itself mirrored the dark sky. He thought he heard a rustling noise behind him and held his breath to listen for more sounds though the echoed heart beat in his ears made it difficult. He waited a minute and decided it was the wind. He slowly emerged from behind his shelter and edged his way along the brush, closer to the sand. He reached the entrance to the sand and peeked his head around the corner. He had a clear view of the beach. It appeared empty as he glanced over to his left then right. He slowly walked onto the sand. He felt his feet sink down as he stepped into the dry sand at the top of the beach. It grew more firm as he walked closer to the water's edge. The area was quiet, except from the noise of the wind that blew harder now across his face as small waves ran up to the tip of his shoes. The beach looked empty, but he couldn't be wrong. He could sense the presence of eyes on him. He turned around and started to walk back to the top of the beach. He paused when he saw a series of grassy dunes that ran along the sand below it for the length of the beach. 'The perfect spot' he thought to himself. Slowly he took a step towards the dunes. He saw the flash of a shadow in his periphery, but was too slow to move. Stevie had bolted from his hiding spot and tackled Andrew hard into the sand. The tackle took him off his feet. They hit the ground locked together and slid to the edge of the water. Andrew's eyes burned from the sand and salt water that shot into his face. His head slapped hard off the firm sand sending a shockwave through his body. He was disoriented and Stevie took the advantage to lock Andrew's arm across his chest. Andrew struggled to free himself while Stevie landed direct blows to his head and face. Andrew tried to avoid them, but his movement was limited. He shut his eyes and dug his chin into his chest. The blows kept coming. He managed to lift his knees, then thrust his hips upward with as much force as he could muster. The force knocked Stevie off balance and Andrew managed to roll to his left quickly and crawled in the sand to create some distance between them. His head ached and he was dizzy. He managed to climb to his feet, but his legs were rubbery. Stevie rushed him again. Andrew rolled with the charge and shifted out of the way at the last second, tripping Stevie with his ankle. He jumped up quickly, while the momentum sent Stevie stumbling into the shallow water. He scrambled to his feet and turned to rush Andrew again. Andrew reached behind him and felt the revolver handle sticking out from his belt. He gripped the handle and pulled the gun out from behind him. Stevie paused, his chest heaving to catch his breath. Andrew stood with his arm outstretched, at the end of it was the revolver. Stevie's eyes moved from the gun up to Andrew's eyes. 'You won't do it Andrew.' He said.

'Tell me where she is Stevie.' Andrew said.

'She's around.' He said. His face turned into a smile.

Andrew winced. 'It was you.' He said. 'It was all you . . . Why Stevie?'

Stevie shook his head. 'What the fuck do you want to hear Andrew?'

Andrew gripped the gun tighter. His index finger danced around the trigger. 'There has to be a reason. You were gonna let me rot in there?' He said.

Stevie shook his head. He took a hesitant step forward. Andrew responded by straightening his arm out further. 'You want to know how I do it Andrew. You want to know all about it? Well I'll tell you. I like to strangle them first to the point where I can just about see the life get ready to leave their eyes. If they shit themselves I cut their throat on the spot and watch them slowly bleed to death. If they only piss themselves, then I fuck 'em first.' He smiled wider and leaned his head forward. He then whispered. 'That the shit you want to hear, you chicken shit. Plus . . . I'm the reason they let you out.'

Andrew felt sick to his stomach. His outstretched arm began to ache. 'He killed Lisa Stark, so the police would know it was wasn't me.' He thought. He felt like he was about to explode. His eyes pleaded with Stevie's. 'Why Stevie? It's me man. We're like brothers.'

Andrew watched Stevie's eyes slowly begin to water. For a moment, he was his longtime best friend again. 'Brothers' Stevie whispered, 'and you left me.' He blinked his watery eyes and looked back at Andrew. 'You knew. You knew who she was. What she did to me . . . over and over. Everyone knew.'

Andrew fought to keep his arm up. He wanted to drop the gun and reach out to Stevie, but he knew that was a mistake. Stevie was right though. Deep down, Andrew did know. He thought of the dark cloud that would come over Stevie whenever she was brought up. 'Stevie . . . your mother?'

Stevie nodded and the tears came back into his eyes, stronger this time. He sniffled, 'no one even asked any questions when she disappeared. That's when I realized for certain . . . everyone knew.'

'Stevie, these girls . . . they are not your mother' Andrew

said in soft tone, 'Gina, Lisa, they were our friends. Not your mother.'

'You don't get Andrew. You can't get it. You never will. They all were her . . . to me . . . all of 'em.'

Andrew's arm finally gave in to the strain and he lowered the gun to his side for the moment. 'Not Bernie. She's not.' 'No' Stevie said. 'Bernie's something else entirely.'

They both remained standing, neither one was prepared to move just yet. Andrew heard rustling noises around him suddenly, but refused to take his eyes off of Stevie. In a panic, he raised the gun up again and kept it fixed on Stevie. He heard a voice yell. 'Dawson! Put the gun down and step aside!' he recognized it immediately. It was Detective Harris's voice.

Andrew kept his gaze fixed on Stevie. 'Harris must have followed my truck. Probably since I left Mackin's' he thought. He yelled back 'You don't know what he's done Detective!'

'I do Andrew. I do know. And he'll pay. Just step aside and put that gun down son.'

Andrew considered what to do next, but made no movement.

'I'm not going with them Andrew.' Stevie whispered to him through gritted teeth. 'I die here today. It might as well be you.'

'Fuck you Stevie.' Andrew said back.

'Fine, be like that, but as soon as you move, they'll shoot. Believe me, they'll shoot.' He said. 'Or I'll make 'em shoot.'

Detective Harris yelled to Andrew again. 'Andrew, please. Listen . . . we have Bernadette Andrew. We found her. She's safe . . . it's over now. Put the gun down.'

'A trick?' Andrew thought. Then a moment later he heard it. Her voice. 'Andrew!' Bernadette yelled. 'Put the gun down please.' She said, her voice straining. 'I'm here . . . . I'm safe now. Please!'

Andrew felt his sinuses loosen. He felt his eyes swell with tears that blurred his vision. 'Her voice' he thought. 'Sweeter than any music on earth.' He looked at Stevie. Stevie smiled at Andrew, willing him to do something, pull the trigger most likely.

Andrew slowly brought his arm down again. He kept his eyes on Stevie while he lowered it. Finally he gripped the gun in his palm, turned and threw it as hard as he could into the water. He heard voices behind him and could hear movement. He assumed the cops staked out with the Detective were moving in. He let out a breath and felt a moment of relief. He dropped his gaze from Stevie for only a moment. It was in that moment, that Stevie stopped smiling. His face turned hard and grew a gross snarl. Andrew looked up at him to see his right hand now held in it a long knife. Andrew shifted his right foot back quickly. He heard shouts from behind him and could feel the sandy ground thunder with pounding footsteps. Had it not happened so fast, he would've had time to think. But, Stevie was always fast, much faster than Andrew at least. Stevie had initiated the action, all Andrew could do was give over control to his body and let his muscles react in the way they had been trained.

Stevie stepped forward quickly. Andrew braced himself. Stevie plunged forward with the knife straight and high, aiming for Andrew's neck. Andrew bounced back from his lead foot shifting his weight to the back and quickly moved his head to the left. He swept the attempted blow past him with his left hand. The forward motion threw Stevie off balance. Andrew shot his right hand out and grabbed Stevie's wrist, which held the knife. He dipped down and drove up with his left shoulder striking underneath Stevie's elbow. The arm hyperextended and Andrew heard a 'pop'. He could feel the strength leave Stevie's arm. He slid his hand from the wrist upwards and pulled the knife away. Andrew gripped the knife tightly, then pivoted with the back foot and plunged the knife straight forward, landing it directly into Stevie's chest.

He looked up and saw Stevie's eyes widen in momentary pain, then go dull as he stumbled backwards. He watched him slowly fall into the sand. Andrew felt hands grabbing him and pulling him back. Voices were talking to him, but he was in a daze and couldn't make out the words. The last thing he saw before he dropped to his knees to get sick was the ring of red slowly starting to form around the handle of the knife that was protruding out of best friend's chest.

CHAPTER TWENTY-NINE

Andrew stood holding onto a pole in the middle of the tram. It was a Friday afternoon and the tram going towards Stephen's Green was wedged with people heading into town. It slid to approach Stephen's Green at the top of Grafton Street and slowed to a stop at the end of the track. The doors chimed twice, and then opened. The people inside flowed out of the doors like water from a broken damn, while still avoiding blocks of people bunched together waiting to climb on going the other way. Andrew squeezed through the people, pushing his way past the tightly packed commuters and spilled out at the entrance to Stephen's Green. He crossed the street and walked the short distance to Dawson Street.

He walked the few blocks and stopped outside of Dawson Street Grille. He stood back and took in the shop front. He had missed the place over the last few weeks. He'd wanted to race back sooner. He would have as soon as he knew Bernie was safe, but Detective Harris insisted he stick around for what he termed 'administrative purposes.' Finally after a few weeks of waiting that included several meetings with cops and lawyers, he was left to continue on with his life. He took in a deep breath then walked up to the door. He twisted the knob and opened it, then slowly entered the restaurant. He could smell food coming from the kitchen that made his mouth water. He looked around the room quickly and saw Donal standing in the bar. He was leaning his elbow against one of the tall tables, talking to Danny Carson who was seated there with a pint of Guinness in front of him. Andrew walked over towards them and nonchalantly cleared his throat. Each man turned and looked over when they heard him. Andrew nodded to them both. Danny Carson smiled and nodded back. Donal waved and said 'Well well. The prodigal son returns. How're you keeping Andrew?'

'I'm good, thanks. I'm uh . . . glad to be back.' He said. Danny pointed at his own face in question, silently asking Andrew about the scars on his cheek. 'You're alright I take it?' he asked.

'This' Andrew pointed. 'Yeah, might scar a little, but I'm fine.'

Both men nodded. By the lack of questions, Andrew assumed they both were aware of what happened in Quincy and that Bernadette was found. She was badly beaten, but she was alive, and now she was safe. He couldn't really say the same for Stevie Black. He was taken into custody and operated on under armed guard at Massachusetts General Hospital. The surgeons were able to save his life. But, there isn't much of a life to be saved. If Detective Harris is to be believed, he'll never again see natural light.

'So . . . Donal' Andrew said. 'I was really hoping I could, you know, get my job back. I know I kind of disappeared on you and let you down. I want you to know I'm sorry.'

Donal looked at him and kept smiling. He shook his head and said, 'Suit up Andrew. We could use you tonight. Go grab an apron and start setting up.'

'Thanks Donal. You don't know what this means to me. I won't let you down again, I promise you that.' He said.

Danny Carson slid his chair back and stood up. 'If you're giving out apologies Andrew, I'm not sure it's Donal you need to start with buddy. If I were you, I'd start with her.' He said pointing into the dining room.

Andrew looked across the room. He saw Vicky. She was busying herself getting ready for the shift. He stared across at her. Her hair was pulled back, and tied up, but the dark curls fell loose in the back. Andrew felt a stir in his stomach. He had forgotten, however briefly, just how powerful her spell over him was. Only now did he truly feel the pain of how much he'd missed her in just those few weeks. She looked up and saw him. Andrew smiled and waved to her. Her face stayed straight. It did not smile. In fact, it showed no emotion at all. She looked down quickly, then walked directly back through the kitchen doors.

Andrew looked back over to Donal and Danny Carson. Both men smiled and shrugged.

'I think you're right Danny.' Andrew said. 'That's where I need to start.'

Paul Garvey grew up in Quincy, Massachusetts and currently lives in Dublin, Ireland. *Green Wings to Eden* is his second novel. His first novel, *Tomorrow's Sun* was released in February 2013.

CPSIA information can be obtained at www.ICGtesting.com
Printed in the USA
LVOW05s1756070414

380671LV00017B/1398/P